Also by Cynthia DeFelice

The Apprenticeship of
Lucas Whitaker

The Ghost of Fossil Glen

The Ghost of Fossil Glen

Cynthia DeFelice

Farrar, Straus and Giroux

NEW YORK

Library of Congress Cataloging-in-Publication Data
DeFelice, Cynthia C.
  The ghost of Fossil Glen / Cynthia DeFelice.—1st ed.
    p.   cm.
  Summary: Allie knows it's not her imagination when she hears a
voice and sees in her mind's eye the face of a girl who seems to be
seeking Allie's help.
  ISBN 0-374-31787-9
  [1. Ghosts—Fiction. 2. Diaries—Fiction. 3. Imagination—Fiction.]
I. Title.
  PZ7.D339255Gh   1998
  [Fic]—dc21   97-33230

For Mary Burke,
friend at first sight and always

The Ghost of Fossil Glen

One

Allie Nichols clung to the side of the steep cliff, trying to calm her racing heart and *think*. Stupidly, the only thought that came to her mind was: Mom and Dad would kill me if they knew where I was right now.

How many times had her mother warned about how dangerous Fossil Glen could be? How many times had her father reminded her not to go fossil hunting alone? How many times had they both cautioned her about climbing too high on the steep shale cliffs that rose perpendicular from the stream bed at the bottom of the glen?

"All the best fossils are up in the cliffs," Allie always told them, which was true. But her parents were right: Fossil Glen could be dangerous, as Allie's predicament clearly proved.

Mom and Dad won't have to kill me, she thought, because I'll already be dead. She felt tears spring to her eyes and almost lifted her hand to brush them away before remembering: she couldn't let go of the large exposed hemlock tree root. It was all that was keeping her from tumbling over one hundred feet straight down.

She couldn't change the position of her feet, either. The tips of her sneakers dug into the crumbly rock of the cliff side. Each time she tried to move, she dislodged several layers of the thin, slippery shale and slid farther downward. She was already stretched as far as she could stretch: her hands clung desperately to the root, her feet dug precariously into the shale, the side of her face pressed into the wall of the cliff.

There she hung, like Allie the Human Fly, except that, unfortunately, she had no wings. She'd thought climbing up was the hard part; now she realized it was even trickier to get back down.

She inched her head to the side so that she could look below her. Her eyes snapped shut when she saw how far away the ground was. She made herself open them again to survey the surface of the cliff beneath her, to see if there was anything down there that she could grab onto if she let go of the root and slid down the cliff side.

If there wasn't, and she fell all the way—well, she didn't want to think about that. But if she managed to get down lower and *then* fell, perhaps she wouldn't do anything worse than break a bone or two.

About halfway to the ground there was another hemlock tree. Thin and scrawny, it grew bravely out from the rocky wall. She had used it to pull herself up; now she hoped that it was strong enough to hold her weight if she grabbed it on the way down.

One by one, she began to uncurl the fingers of one fist. But then she froze. It was just too scary to let go.

Suddenly, from somewhere, she heard a voice. It wasn't a voice she recognized and yet it seemed familiar. It was soft and soothing and seemed to be coming from inside her head. She trusted it right away.

"*Go ahead,*" said the voice. "*Let go. You can do it.*"

A feeling of calmness and confidence began to come over Allie.

"*It will be all right.*"

Allie believed the voice. Still, she hesitated.

"*Now. Before you're so tired you simply fall.*"

Yes, thought Allie. Now. Letting go of the root first with one hand and then with the other, she began to slide down the face of the cliff, slowly at first and then faster. She ignored the terrible clatter of falling rock and the scraping of her hands and face and concentrated on the skinny hemlock trunk. She reached for it, caught it, and held on with all her might.

Her arms were nearly jerked from her shoulder sockets, but she held on and, miraculously, the little tree's roots held fast in the stony soil. Her right foot found a narrow ledge. Carefully, she tested her weight on it. It was solid. She brought her left foot next to her right.

In this position, which was far more secure, she rested for a moment before looking down. The ground was closer, though still far away.

"*Good,*" said the voice. "*Now slide. Don't lean back. Just let yourself slide.*"

Again, Allie did what the voice told her to do. She let go and slid. When she hit the ground, her legs buckled under her. She landed on her bottom and then on her back, in a cascade of rocks and dirt.

"Ow!" she moaned. She sat up and gingerly examined the damage. Her rear end hurt—a lot. Her hands were scraped and raw. Her face felt just like her hands. She reached up to touch her cheek and her finger came away bloody, but she couldn't tell if the blood came from her face or her hand. Probably both, she thought.

Allie stood up, brushing the dirt from her clothing. There was a rip in the front of her windbreaker, and her sneakers were full of dirt and stones. Her right elbow hurt where she had used it to soften the force of her fall. But nothing was broken. She was alive.

Glancing up, she saw the place where she had been clinging desperately just minutes before. Her heart lurched. Feeling dizzy and slightly sick, she realized how close she had come to serious injury or even death. She took a deep breath and looked away.

Still feeling shaky, Allie began walking downstream to the path that led out of the glen. From the back pocket of her jeans, she took out the trilobite, the treasure that had gotten her into trouble in the first place. It was when she had reached back to put it in her pocket that she had lost her balance and made her first terrifying slide down the cliff.

She looked with satisfaction at the fossilized remains of the extinct marine animal. It was a beauty, all right. She had found not just a part but the ancient creature's entire body. She couldn't help smiling. Now that she had both feet firmly on the ground, she thought the fossil was well worth the risk she had taken. It was the prize specimen of her collection.

For as long as Allie could remember, she had been fascinated with fossils. They were reminders of a world that had existed long before she was born, an undersea world that was almost impossible to imagine. And yet she held proof of it right in her hand.

She had tried to get her two best girlfriends, Karen and Pam, interested in fossils, but every time she talked about her hobby, they looked at her as if she was crazy. "You call that fun?" Karen said. "Climbing around in the glen, getting all dirty? And for what? Little hunks of rock?"

Wait until I tell them about today's adventure, Allie thought. Wait until I show them this trilobite. Wait until I tell them how that voice just came to me and told me what to do.

Suddenly she stopped short. *The voice*. How could she have forgotten? With a puzzled frown, she searched her memory. Whose voice had it been? She tried to recall what it had said. The exact words were gone, but she remembered distinctly the reassurance she had felt, the calmness and courage the voice had given her.

She had been alone on the cliff. Still, she'd heard the voice. It had come from somewhere. It had belonged to someone. It had saved her life, she realized. But no matter how she tried, she couldn't imagine whose voice it had been, or how it had gotten inside her head.

Two

Allie walked home in a daze, contemplating her odd experience at the glen. As usual, she stopped to check the mailbox before walking up the driveway to her house. When she reached into the box, a peculiar tingling feeling ran down the length of her arm and all through her body. It felt almost as if she'd stuck her finger into an electric socket.

"Yikes!" With a yelp, she jumped back and withdrew her hand.

She looked around her. Everything appeared normal on Cumberland Road: houses, lawns, trees, and mailboxes lined the quiet street. Warily, she stared again at her own family's mailbox. The door hung open and a cold dampness poured from its wide-open mouth. Allie shivered despite the warm afternoon sun.

A voice whispered softly. It was the same voice she'd heard in the glen, except this time the words were muffled and unclear. She whirled around to see who'd come sneaking up behind her. There was no one in sight.

She stood for a moment, perplexed. Then, cautiously, she reached once again into the box. As she pulled out the thick bundle of letters, magazines, and glossy flyers, there was no mistaking the feeling that came over her. Again, her skin prickled, her fingers grew cold and clammy, and her heart beat loudly in her chest. And again she heard the voice, a whisper so faint it seemed to be coming from inside her own head.

"At last," the voice said, *"the time has come."*

At least that was what Allie thought it said. She couldn't be sure.

The shrill ring of the telephone came from the open window of her house. Allie slammed the mailbox shut and ran inside.

Tossing the mail onto the counter, she grabbed for the phone. "Hello," she said breathlessly.

"Hi, Al. It's me."

"Oh, hi, Dub," Allie said.

"Where have you been? I've been calling for an hour."

"I was in the glen. I found an incredible fossil, Dub. A whole trilobite, a pretty big one."

"Cool. Bring it to school tomorrow so I can see it."

"Okay. So what's up?"

"My dad's using the computer, so I don't have anything to do."

Allie laughed. She liked to tease Dub about being a cyberhead because of all the hours he spent on his computer. "Thanks a lot. You mean you called me because you were bored."

"Actually, I was calling to procrastinate," Dub said. "I can't think of anything to write in my journal."

Allie groaned. "Well, you're ahead of me. I don't even *have* a journal yet."

"Mr. Henry said it's okay to use a regular notebook," said Dub.

"I know, but I forgot to get one," Allie said. "I'm not sure there's anything like that around here, and Mom's going to kill me if she has to drive back into town tonight to buy a notebook."

She looked around the kitchen. There was a chunky memo pad on the counter that the family used to leave one another messages, but that wouldn't do. Idly, she began to look through the pile of mail.

"You'd better find something," said Dub. "We're supposed to hand in our journals tomorrow with our first entries done."

Allie's attention was caught by a package wrapped in white tissue paper and tied with red ribbon. When she picked it up, the peculiar quivery feeling hummed through her again. Turning the package over, she discovered with surprise that her name was written on the front. Just Allie—no last name, no address. The writing was large and neat and looping.

It was April; her birthday wasn't for another two months. She searched the outside of the package for clues but found nothing to indicate who had left it for her.

"Yo, Allie. Hello?" Dub asked.

"Sorry. I was looking at this thing that came with the mail."

"What is it?"

"Hang on. I haven't opened it yet. I've got to get some scissors."

Wedging the phone between her ear and her shoulder, Allie rummaged in the junk drawer until she found the big kitchen shears, which she used to cut through the ribbon. Carefully, she unfolded the tissue paper.

"Well? What is it?" Dub asked again.

"I'm not sure," said Allie. "Some kind of book." The cover was made of deep red burnished leather, embossed with an elegant patterned border. The pages were edged in gold and there was a red satin ribbon, bound right in with the pages, to use as a place marker. The leather felt rich and smooth, and its pungent smell filled Allie's nostrils.

"What's it called?" asked Dub.

There was no title printed on the cover. Allie examined the spine. Nothing. "I don't know," she answered.

"Open it," urged Dub.

"I am," said Allie. "It's empty. The pages are blank." She turned the pages, feeling the dry, nubby thickness of the paper. The odd, shivery feeling returned, seeming to gather in the pit of her stomach.

"Who's it from?" asked Dub.

"I don't know," said Allie. She flipped through the book, but nothing was written anywhere inside. She looked at the wrapping paper again. "There's no note and no return address."

"Looks like you have a secret admirer," Dub said slyly.

"Oh, sure."

"Hey!" Dub said, his voice brightening. "You can use it for your journal. The pages are blank, right?"

"Yes," Allie said. "But, Dub . . ."

"Yeah?"

"Don't you think it's kind of strange?"

"What?"

"What do you mean, what? You and I are talking about how I need a journal, and this empty book just happens to show up."

"Coincidence, I guess," said Dub. "A lucky one for you."

"Maybe. But . . ." Allie hesitated, trying to think how to explain her feeling that something decidedly unusual was going on. "If I tell you what happened to me today, do you promise you won't think I'm crazy?"

"Too late for that, Al," said Dub cheerfully.

Ignoring this last remark, Allie said, "Dub, when I was in the glen today, I climbed up the cliffs. Pretty high. Well, really high. And I got sort of trapped there. I couldn't go up or down and my arms were really tired and I thought I was going to die."

"Wow," said Dub. "How'd you get down?"

"This is the weird part. I heard this *voice*, Dub. It told me what to do. And all of a sudden I didn't feel scared and I slid down, and I was okay." Holding the phone between her ear and her shoulder again, she examined her palms. They were dirty and scratched and sore. "Well, mostly okay," she added.

"Whose voice was it?" Dub asked curiously.

"I don't know. I mean, there wasn't anybody there. But the voice seemed—familiar, somehow. It was almost as if it came from inside my head, but it wasn't me."

Dub was quiet, listening, so Allie went on. "Then when I got home I opened the mailbox the way I always do, and I got the queerest feeling. You know how people say, Chills ran down my spine? That's exactly what it was like. I heard the voice again, too, but no one was around. And then this book showed up, with my name on the wrapper, and I have no idea who it's from."

"And the book was in the mailbox?" asked Dub.

"Right."

"Cool."

"Dub! This is *serious*!"

"Well, it's weird, I have to agree."

There was silence for a moment.

"You sure it wasn't Michael tricking you?" Dub asked. Michael was Allie's little brother.

"How? He's not home from the baby-sitter's yet," said Allie. "No one's home but me. And don't tell me it was my imagination!"

"Okay," said Dub, "it happened. I guess you'll just have to wait and see if it happens again."

"Mmmmm," Allie agreed.

"So, meanwhile, are you going to use that book for your journal?"

Allie looked again at the dark red leather cover and the gilded pages. "Well, it beats a regular old notebook any day."

"What are you going to write about?"

"I don't know," said Allie.

Dub and Allie were both in Mr. Henry's sixth-grade class. Mr. Henry had announced that everyone was to begin keeping a journal. They could write about anything they pleased—the books they'd read, their daydreams, stories, poems, questions, even their most secret thoughts.

The whole class had agreed on a rule: all journals

were absolutely, positively private. No student was allowed to read anyone else's without permission. The books would be turned in to Mr. Henry from time to time; he alone would read them. "And my lips are sealed," he'd said with a smile, making the motion of locking his mouth and throwing away the key.

Allie rubbed her hand across the smooth leather on the front of the book, thinking.

"Well, I can see you're not going to be much help," said Dub. "I'm hanging up. Hey! Don't forget, tomorrow's Earth Day."

"I won't," said Allie.

Allie's school was going all-out for Earth Day. Each class had selected a special project designed to help the environment and beautify the school and the community. Mr. Henry's class had voted to clean up Fossil Glen Cemetery, which was behind the school about a hundred yards from the steep ravine of Fossil Glen and the creek that ran through its bottom.

"Okay. See you tomorrow," Dub said.

Allie hung up the phone and stood at the kitchen counter, looking at the book. It really *was* beautiful. No one in the class would have a journal anywhere near as special.

She closed her eyes and, hugging the book to her chest, imagined filling it with words that would shine with wit and truth and beauty. Then, as suddenly as before, the chill settled over her, raising the flesh along her arms and all the little hairs on the back of her neck.

Her eyes were still closed when a face appeared in her mind's eye. It was a girl about her own age. The girl's curly black hair floated around her face in a cloud, and her dark eyes penetrated Allie's. Her expression was serious, almost stern, but at the same time sad. The outlines of her image were faint and wispy, as if she were surrounded by fog or mist. Her upper body appeared for a moment, the arms reaching beseechingly toward Allie. Her lips moved slowly, and Allie heard the muted voice. This time the words were distinct, although they sounded as if they came from very far away: *"Help me."* Then the image faded entirely.

Allie had never seen the girl before in her life.

Three

Allie opened her eyes and was glad to find herself alone in the quiet, familiar kitchen, and no sign of a black-haired girl crying for help. She reached for the phone and dialed her friend Karen's number.

"Karen?" she said excitedly. "It's me."

"Oh, hi, Allie. What's up?"

"The strangest thing just happened!"

"What?" said Karen flatly.

"You won't believe it."

Karen muttered, "You got that right."

"What?" said Allie, taken aback by Karen's sarcastic tone.

"Nothing," Karen said. "So what happened?"

Allie was so eager to tell her story that she went on,

despite Karen's odd remark. "I was in the glen today, looking for fossils—"

"Whoopee," Karen broke in.

"I found a good one," Allie said.

"That's what you called to tell me?" asked Karen.

"*No,*" said Allie. "I'm getting to that. I climbed up the cliff pretty high, and I got stuck, and this *voice* spoke to me and told me how to get down, and then when I got home I heard it again and—"

"Who was it?" asked Karen, sounding faintly bored.

"That's what's so strange," Allie said. "There wasn't anybody there." She paused dramatically, waiting for Karen to react with interest to this startling news, or to ask a question, the way Dub had.

The pause grew longer. Finally Karen said, "Here we go. Now you're hearing voices."

Allie stared at the phone, bewildered. "What do you mean?" she asked.

"Oh, never mind," said Karen breezily. "Forget I said anything."

"Wait a second," Allie insisted. "What did you mean?"

"Really, it's nothing," said Karen, "just something Pam and I were talking about after school."

"You were talking about *me*?"

"Yes."

Allie could feel her heart pounding unpleasantly. "What—what were you saying?" she managed to ask.

"Well, nothing personal, but we were saying how you always, you know . . ."

"W-what?" stammered Allie.

"You're, like, such a *liar.*"

Allie's cheeks flooded with a mixture of surprise and embarrassment. "I am not!" she said loudly.

Karen went on as if Allie hadn't spoken. "I wasn't going to say anything, but since you insisted, I'll tell you: we're totally sick of the way you act like everything is so exciting and amazing and interesting all the time. Like there's anything exciting or interesting going on around this boring place."

"I-I don't know what you mean." Allie's voice was almost a whisper.

"Come on, Allie, sure you do. Like today at lunch. All that stuff you were saying about Ms. Gillespie? And Mr. Pinkney and Mrs. Hobbs?"

Allie thought for a moment. She and Karen and Pam had been sitting together in the cafeteria. While they were eating, Ms. Gillespie, the school principal, had walked through the room. Karen had made a remark about Ms. Gillespie's red high heels and her long, red-lacquered fingernails. And Allie, agreeing that Ms. Gillespie was awfully glamorous for a principal, had suggested that perhaps the leader of their school was truly an heiress, disowned by her wealthy family because they disapproved of the man she wanted to marry.

Then, Allie recalled, she had jokingly said that maybe Ms. Gillespie's fiancé disappeared as soon as he found out she'd lost her money, and that *that* was how she had ended up as principal of Seneca Heights School.

"But, Karen," she protested. "I was just kidding around. We all were . . ." Her voice fell off, full of doubt and confusion. "At least, I thought we were."

"What about Mr. Pinkney?" Karen asked accusingly.

Allie had simply been trying to figure out why a man like Mr. Pinkney, who was so out of shape that he huffed and puffed just walking across the room, was working as a gym teacher.

"You *said* he witnessed a murder and now he's hiding out because the murderers want to kill him, too. You said that's why he took on the identity of a gym teacher."

"No, I didn't. I said *maybe*. I was just messing around, playing a game. *Imagining* that it was something like that," explained Allie.

"And what about Mrs. Hobbs and her terrible tragedy?" Karen went on relentlessly.

Mrs. Hobbs was the head cafeteria lady. All the kids, even the sixth-graders, were terrified of her. She stood behind the lunch counter, mouth clamped like an angry snapping turtle, as the children crept fearfully past. A lot of them brought their lunch from home, even on Fridays when there was pizza, rather than have to face her.

"All I said was, I bet that sometime in her past something awful happened to make her so crabby. Maybe it had to do with kids. Don't you think that's possible?" Allie asked, hating the way her voice sounded so small and pleading.

"Who knows?" Karen said breezily. "Who cares? The point is, Pam and I decided we're totally sick of the way you make up stuff like that all the time."

Allie was too stunned to reply.

"No offense, okay?" said Karen. "I'm only telling you as a friend."

Then why didn't it feel friendly? Allie wondered. She opened her mouth, but nothing came out. What was there to say?

"Anyway, I've got to go," Karen said. "I want to get my journal entry done so I can watch *Teen Twins* tonight. I've *got* to find out if Jason likes Jodi or Stephanie. See ya."

There was a click in Allie's ear as Karen hung up. Allie stood in the kitchen, clutching the phone, her cheeks still burning. She started to call Karen back, to correct what was surely a silly misunderstanding, but the memory of Karen's scornful voice made her draw her hand back.

"I wasn't lying," she said fiercely, fighting back tears. "How can she call it that?"

Ever since she was a little girl, Allie had made up stories about the things and the people around her. She knew that there was more to people than their normal, everyday manner revealed. Beneath the surface, the most ordinary objects and people pulsed with extraordinary drama. If you paid attention, she knew, you could see into those hidden truths. Allie paid attention.

And so of course she noticed people, including the teachers at school. And naturally she was curious about Ms. Gillespie, who seemed out of place at Seneca Heights School, and about Mr. Pinkney, who was clearly unsuited for his job as gym teacher, and about Mrs. Hobbs, who plainly hated children. All Allie had been doing was wondering what their lives were like outside of school.

Allie's report cards almost always contained comments about her "active imagination." Sometimes the teachers' words carefully suggested that Allie didn't always know the difference between what was real and what she imagined. But that wasn't right: she knew.

Angrily, she brushed the tears from her eyes, glad that Karen wasn't present to see the effect of her words. Karen was popular, and Allie considered herself lucky to be among Karen's small group of chosen friends. But it was confusing, too. Having friends was supposed to make you feel good. Still, lots of times when Allie was with Karen, she felt the way she did now: unsure, small, as if something was wrong with her.

She thought about how she might make up with Karen at school the next day. She had noticed that Pam pretty much did whatever Karen said. If Karen decided Allie was okay, Pam would go along with her. Every night, Karen and Pam watched *Teen Twins,* Karen's favorite show, and every day they talked about the show and what had happened on it. Allie decided she'd watch that evening so she could join in the discussion the next morning. Then perhaps she could explain that she'd been joking, not lying, and they'd all laugh about the misunderstanding.

She was glad she hadn't told Karen any more about the voice or the mailbox or the mysterious book. She had told Dub, but that was different. Dub had always been around, ever since the first day of kindergarten, when their teacher, Mrs. Uhler, had said, "Raise your hand if you can tie your own shoes." Dub and Allie were the only two kids whose hands didn't go up. Mrs. Uhler sent them into the corner with a big wooden shoe with long red laces so they could practice. The friendship that began over that shoe had continued right into sixth grade.

They were still friends, even though some kids teased them about being secretly "in love," and even

24

though Karen kept asking Allie why she hung around
with a geek like Dub.

But to Allie, Dub wasn't a geek. Dub was—well,
Dub was Dub. Good old Dub.

Four

Allie looked at the kitchen clock and saw that it was 5:30. Her father was probably picking up Michael at the baby-sitter's, which meant they'd be home any minute. She decided to take the red leather book to her room, where it would be safe from Michael and from the mess that often went along with her father's dinner preparations. Gingerly, she picked it up and instantly felt the strange sensation pass through her. In a funny way, it was beginning to seem less scary, more familiar.

She set the book down on the piece of plywood supported by cinder blocks that served as her desk. The sound of Michael's feet running up the stairs was accompanied by her father's voice: "Allie-Cat? We're home."

Allie-Cat was her dad's pet name for her. Sometimes she complained, but the truth was, she liked when he called her that.

Dub was a nickname, too. His real name was his father's, Oliver James Whitwell, but his mother had always called him Dub, short for "double." She said it was to save him from being stuck with Ollie or Junior. Dub was grateful, and Allie could see why.

"Hi, Dad. Be right down."

Michael appeared at the door to her bedroom, saying, "Guess what I—" He stopped, staring wide-eyed at Allie.

"What's the matter, Mikey?" said Allie, laughing at the expression on his face. "You look like you saw a ghost!"

"You look funny," said Michael. He sounded scared.

"What do you mean?" asked Allie. She glanced in the mirror over her dresser and gasped. There were two red stripes of blood across her cheek, where she had rubbed her face with her bleeding fingers. More blood had dripped from her forehead down to her eyebrow, where it had caked and dried, and some was smeared on the front of her windbreaker, which was ripped and covered with dirt. Her hair was sticking out of her barrettes in wild disarray, and the knees of her pants were torn and filthy.

She knelt down in front of Michael and smiled at

him. "It's okay, Mike. I just got dirty looking for fossils, and cut myself a little bit. I'm a mess, huh?"

Michael nodded solemnly. Allie pointed to the front of Michael's shirt, which was spattered with red, yellow, blue, and brown paint. "You're kind of a mess yourself, squirt," she said.

Michael's face broke into a grin. "Guess what I did at Fritzi's today?"

Fritzi was Michael's baby-sitter. Looking at Michael, Allie was pretty sure she knew, but she asked anyway. "What?"

"Painted," said Michael proudly.

"What did you paint? Besides yourself."

"Pictures," Michael answered. "Fritzi had big, big paper and we covered the whole thing."

"Sounds like fun," said Allie. "I just heard Mom come in. How 'bout we clean up a little bit before dinner?"

Allie scrubbed Michael's face and arms, and found him a clean shirt. Then she dabbed carefully at her own face with a washcloth. With the blood gone and her hair combed to hide the cut above her eye, she didn't look bad at all. She put on a clean shirt and changed into a different pair of jeans, then checked herself in the mirror and felt satisfied that her appearance wouldn't cause her parents any alarm.

She sprayed some cleanser on the spots of paint and blood, and was just putting the dirty clothes into the hamper when she heard her mother call up the stairs: "Allie! Michael! Dinner's ready."

As the family ate the leftover spaghetti and meatballs Mr. Nichols had hastily popped in the microwave, Mrs. Nichols told them about her day at the antiques shop she owned in town. "A man stopped by today, saying he was in charge of selling the contents of the Stiles house."

At the mention of the Stiles house, Allie's ears perked up. She walked by the deserted Stiles house twice each day, since it was just three doors down from school. For years, it had been empty. As time passed, it grew more and more bleak and desolate-looking. The white paint was faded and peeling, the porch was crumpling wearily, and the loose black shutters banged noisily in the wind. The grass, untended, was overgrown and had given way in places to various weeds and vines, some of which climbed the columns on the porch, adding to the dreary sense of abandonment.

For Allie, the place held a creepy fascination. She couldn't help wondering what had happened to the Stiles family. Where had they gone, and why? Why did the house remain empty and unsold? She'd made up fascinating stories about the people, now gone, who had lived there.

"Naturally, I was curious," Mrs. Nichols was saying. "I've always heard the house was beautifully furnished, and that everything was simply left there. I told him I'd take a look at what he had. We went out to his van, where he had some really exquisite pieces. I ended up buying quite a few."

"That's a bit unusual, isn't it?" asked Mr. Nichols.

"Well, yes," said Mrs. Nichols. "I guess that's why I mentioned it. Most of the time, I buy from auctions or estate sales or shows. I don't believe I've ever had anyone drop by like that, selling from the back of a van. But he had all the proper ownership papers and so on."

"Was it Mr. Stiles?" asked Allie.

"No," answered her mother. "I believe Mr. Stiles died some time ago. This man's name was Curtis. The papers said he was the agent for somebody else. I can't remember the name."

"Is someone moving into the house?" asked Mr. Nichols. "Is that why they're selling off the contents?"

"I asked Mr. Curtis that," said Mrs. Nichols, "but he didn't seem to know anything. He'd been hired to empty the place out, that's all."

She turned eagerly to Allie. "I bought a desk, sweetie, that's really quite special. I thought you might want it for your room. You should come by and take a look at it."

"Okay, Mom."

"It's about time we got you something to replace that piece of plywood you've been using," said Mrs. Nichols with a smile.

When they had finished talking and eating, Allie excused herself to do her homework. She shut her bedroom door so Michael wouldn't come in and bother her. She wanted complete privacy to concentrate on her first journal entry. Slowly, she walked toward her desk, anticipating the thrilling, disquieting feeling she'd had earlier. But she felt nothing unusual.

Relieved, and a little disappointed, she sat down to write. She wanted to write something that would dazzle Mr. Henry with her creativity and brilliance. But her brain felt empty as she looked at the clean, blank journal pages. Nothing at all came to mind.

She looked at her pen. It was an ordinary ballpoint. Not, she thought, very inspiring, definitely not a proper pen for writing something momentous. She closed the book, got up, went down the hall to the room her parents used for an office, and rummaged in the desk drawer until she came upon her mother's fountain pen and the bottle of peacock-blue ink. That, she thought with satisfaction, was what she needed.

When she got back to her room, the door was closed. "Michael?" she said, stepping into the room. "Are you in here?"

No answer.

"Come on, Michael. Quit fooling around. I've got homework to do." She checked the only two places where he could be hiding, the closet and under the bed, but there was no sign of Michael.

Her heart lurched. The book was *open*. She was sure she had closed it before leaving the room.

Then she saw the gold-edged pages of her journal flutter just a bit. She looked toward the window. It was shut. A slight breeze came through the doorway, but it wasn't strong enough to open the heavy leather cover and blow the pages about.

The air in the bedroom felt chilly. Allie's eyes fell on the journal, open to the first page. Legs trembling, she walked closer.

The page was no longer blank. Written at the top in a thin, quavering hand were the words:

I am L

Allie stared at the page in wonder. The "L" trailed off in a streak of ink, as if the writer had been interrupted suddenly, or as if the effort of writing had been too great. But who could it have been?

Taking a deep breath, she told herself that there was one obvious explanation: the words had been there before and she simply hadn't seen them. She recalled looking through every page of the book as she'd talked with Dub on the phone. Had she somehow missed the first page? She didn't think so.

She looked again at the message. Who was "L"? She had no idea.

Five

Allie called down the stairs, "Mom! Dad! Can you come up here?"

Her parents came to the bedroom door. "What's up, Allie-Cat?" said her father.

"Look!" said Allie excitedly, pointing to the page in her journal with the words, "I am L."

Mr. and Mrs. Nichols looked at the book, then gazed at Allie questioningly. "What?" asked her mother.

Allie explained about the peculiar sensation she'd felt at the mailbox and the odd appearance of the book she was using for her journal. She left out the part about the voice, not wanting to worry her parents with the story of her near-disaster in Fossil Glen. She told about leaving the room and returning to find the message.

"Hold on a second," said her father. "This book just came out of the blue? In the mail?"

"It was in the box when I got home," Allie said. "It was wrapped like a present, in white tissue paper and red ribbon. My name was written on the paper."

"I don't understand it," said Mrs. Nichols. "How did it get there?"

Allie shrugged.

"And you're saying it was completely blank when you left the room for a minute, and then those words somehow appeared?" asked her mother.

"Yes!" Allie nodded. "Pretty weird, huh?"

Allie's parents exchanged a glance. Her mother said, "Well, we know the book didn't come through the mail. Somebody must have put it there."

"I know, but who?" asked Allie. "And who wrote in it just now?"

"Well, your father and Michael and I were downstairs in the living room," her mother went on logically. "So the writing must have been in the book all along, and when you flipped through the pages, you didn't see it."

"I thought of that," said Allie. "But I'm sure it wasn't there before."

"Then how would you explain what happened?" asked her father.

"I don't know. How would *you* explain it?" Allie asked.

"I think," said Mr. Nichols slowly, "it's possible that a certain creative young lady with a desire for excitement might have concocted an interesting story to write about in her journal." He looked at Allie with a teasing smile. "Is there any chance of that?"

Karen's accusation flashed through Allie's mind: *Pam and I decided we're totally sick of the way you make up stuff all the time.* "No!" Allie nearly shouted. "I didn't make it up!"

"Allie, honey," said her mother, "your father and I are wondering if maybe your imagination is running away with you."

"I told you," said Allie stubbornly. "I didn't make it up."

There was an uncomfortable silence. Allie could tell that her mother and father were sending those invisible parent communication vibes back and forth, deciding who would speak next. Her father cleared his throat and said, "Well. I'm sure there's some kind of logical, rational explanation for all this. Maybe one of your friends left the book and meant to enclose a note or something. Whoever it was will probably let you know. Let's wait and see."

"Good idea," Allie said quickly. "Let's wait and see."

When her parents left the room, Allie sighed. She

supposed she couldn't really blame them for their skepticism. Maybe there was, as her father believed, a logical, rational explanation. But Allie *knew* that those words had not been in the book before. She didn't know how they'd gotten there, or why, but she was going to try to find out.

At least, she thought excitedly, her father had given her an idea for her first journal entry. She could write about the strange message. Mr. Henry had told the class to be creative and daring. Well, her entry would be unique—she was pretty sure of that.

Eagerly, using her mother's fountain pen to form her letters as neatly as she could, Allie began to write. When she was finished, she looked at the clock. Eight-fifteen. She could catch the last half of *Teen Twins* if she hurried downstairs.

She turned on the television in the family room. The faces of Stephanie and Jodi, the twins, filled the screen. They were in a school hallway, hiding behind a locker door, watching as another girl opened her locker and looked inside. The girl picked up a note and read it. Her expression showed surprise followed by great happiness. The camera zoomed in on the note, which said, "I love you," and was signed, "Brian."

The girl folded the note and placed it carefully in her backpack, closed her locker, and walked down the hall. Her face glowed with pleasure.

The picture shifted to Stephanie and Jodi, who were

collapsing with laughter as they emerged from their hiding place. "She fell for it!" Jodi exclaimed.

"Like Brian would ever love *her*!" said Stephanie with a giggle.

Allie frowned. She hadn't seen the beginning of the show, but it appeared that the twins were playing a joke on the other girl. A cruel joke, it seemed to Allie, one that was purposely designed to embarrass their victim. She didn't get it: was it supposed to be funny? She stood up and turned off the television, not really caring to see what happened next.

Six

In the morning, Allie walked downstairs to find Michael and her parents finishing breakfast.

"There's some toast here, Allie-Cat," said her father.

"Thanks, Dad," said Allie. Taking her seat, she reached for a piece of toast and asked, "Is it all right if I take a rake and a broom and some trash bags to school for Earth Day?"

Michael banged his cereal spoon on the table enthusiastically. "Earth Day!" he crowed. "Fritzi and me are going to plant flowers today!"

"Fritzi and *I* are going to plant flowers," Mrs. Nichols corrected gently.

Michael's round face gathered in a scowl. "No!" he protested. *"Not you. Me!* Fritzi said."

"That's right, honey," Mrs. Nichols hastened to say. "You and Fritzi are planting flowers. I just meant—Oh, never mind."

Michael smiled happily. Mr. Nichols turned back to Allie and said, "Sure, go ahead and take whatever tools you need. What are you going to use them for?"

"We're cleaning up the cemetery at Fossil Glen today," answered Allie.

Mr. Nichols nodded approvingly. "Good idea."

"If you're going to be carrying all that, why don't you let me give you a ride?" asked Mrs. Nichols.

"Great, Mom," said Allie. "Thanks."

"Go brush your teeth, and I'll meet you in the car."

As Allie and her mother drove past the Stiles house, Mrs. Nichols said, "Why, that's Mr. Curtis's van in the driveway. There must be more furniture to move out."

Ordinarily, Allie would have been interested in any sign of life at the Stiles house, but she had spotted Karen Laver and Pam Wright walking to school. They were headed toward the place where her mother would pull up to drop her off.

A little knot of anxiety began to form in the pit of Allie's stomach. "Mom," she said quickly, "this is good enough. Stop here."

"But, honey, I have to pull into the parking lot to turn around, anyway." Mrs. Nichols kept driving, right up to the front door of the school, where she stopped.

"Thanks a lot," Allie said glumly.

"Have a good day, sweetie. And stop by the shop after school if you can. I'd like you to see that desk."

"Okay," said Allie. But she didn't move. She calculated that if she stalled for just a minute, Karen and Pam would be inside the building before she got out of the car. Since both girls were in her class, she'd have to face them soon. But it would be better in the classroom, with all the other kids and Mr. Henry around.

"Oh, look," said Mrs. Nichols, "I see Karen and Pam." She raised her arm to wave.

"No, Mom. Don't." Allie sank down low in the seat.

Mrs. Nichols turned to Allie, a puzzled look on her face. "What's the matter? They're your friends."

"Yeah," said Allie unhappily. She watched as Karen and Pam disappeared into the building, laughing together.

"Is something wrong?" Mrs. Nichols asked.

"No."

"Are you sure?"

"Yeah. Everything's fine."

Mrs. Nichols looked at Allie questioningly, and Allie could see that her mother was waiting for a better answer than that. She tried to make her voice breezy and carefree. "Karen told me yesterday that she and Pam were talking about me. She said that, as my friend, she thought she should let me know . . ."

"Know what, sweetie?"

"That they think I'm a liar," Allie said quickly, the words coming all at once in a rush.

"Why would they think that?" said Mrs. Nichols indignantly.

Allie shrugged.

"No reason?" asked Mrs. Nichols.

Allie sighed. Finally, in a low voice, she said, "They think I make stuff up. But I don't!"

Mrs. Nichols lifted her eyebrows. "Because sometimes you let your imagination run away with you?" she suggested gently.

Miserably, Allie said, "Well, that's what you and Dad call it, anyway."

Her mother sighed. "Allie, honey, we've been through this before, haven't we? I know you don't mean any harm when you make up your stories. You get carried away. Like last night, with that business about your journal—" She stopped when she saw Allie's face.

"You think I'm a liar, too, then!" shouted Allie.

Her mother reached over to touch her cheek. "No, sweetie, I just think that—"

A loud bell rang, signaling that students were to be in their homerooms.

"I've got to go," Allie said.

"I hate to have you go into school so upset, Al. Are you going to be all right?"

Allie nodded.

"We'll talk more tonight," Mrs. Nichols said. "Okay?"

"Sure, Mom. Bye." Allie took the tools from the back seat and walked up the path to school, aware that her mother was still sitting in the car, watching her.

Seven

Mr. Henry's classroom was humming with excitement and activity when Allie walked in. Rakes, shovels, edging tools, clippers, and trash bags were piled near the door. All the kids were dressed, as Allie was, for working outside. Mr. Henry was wearing jeans, a denim shirt, and worn leather boots.

Allie saw Karen and Pam standing over by the cage that held Butterscotch, the class guinea pig. She took a deep breath and started toward them, but Dub caught her sleeve as she passed his desk. "Did you remember the trilobite?" he asked.

"Yeah!" said Allie, and she reached eagerly into the pocket of her jeans. "Look!"

Dub took the fossil from her hand and whistled

softly with admiration. Some other kids came over to see what Dub was looking at and began asking questions.

"What is it?"

"Where'd you get it?"

"Can I see?"

Dub was passing the trilobite around and Allie was explaining what it was, when Karen and Pam joined the group. Karen took a look and wrinkled up her nose. "Oh, it's another one of your little rocks," she said, sounding bored. "I thought it was something interesting." Then she sauntered over to her desk as Mr. Henry turned the lights off, then back on, the signal for everyone to stop talking and sit down.

Allie sat at her desk, all the pleasure of showing her fossil draining away.

When the class was quiet, Mr. Henry smiled and said, "Before we head over to the cemetery, I'd like to collect your journals, so would you please pass them forward?" He continued talking while desktops and backpacks were opened, and journals were retrieved and passed forward. "I'll read these tonight and return them to you tomorrow. Any problems or questions about journals before we go?"

Joey Fratto raised his hand. "I forgot mine," he said.

Mr. Henry thumped his forehead with his palm in mock despair. "Joey, Joey, Joey, how many times have we talked about this?" He paused. "You'll bring it tomorrow?"

Joey nodded.

"Without fail?"

Joey smiled sheepishly. "Yeah."

Mr. Henry made his face very stern, but everyone in the class knew he was only pretending to be mad. *"Or else.* And you don't want to find out what I mean by that, do you?"

Joey shook his head. He was grinning, but Allie was willing to bet that Joey would remember his journal the next day. Mr. Henry had a way of getting kids to follow the rules without making a big deal about it.

"Anyone else?" Mr. Henry asked.

Karen raised her hand. "You said nobody is going to read them except you, right?"

"Class, we all took the oath of secrecy, didn't we?" said Mr. Henry.

"Yes," everyone chorused.

"So your journals are safe in this room," said Mr. Henry. "And they'll be safe at my house as well, because Hoover is much more interested in chewing up pillows and drinking out of the toilet bowl than in reading journals. Okay?"

Several kids laughed, and Karen looked satisfied. Hoover was Mr. Henry's golden retriever. Mr. Henry told stories about her all the time, and even brought her to school sometimes. She was the official class mascot.

Mr. Henry was young and unmarried and, Allie thought, handsome. The kids were always trying to worm information out of him about his girlfriend. He always answered by saying, "Ah, you mean Miss Hoover," and began recounting one of his dog's latest misdeeds or amazing accomplishments.

He'd told them, for instance, that, the week before, she had dug up his neighbor's entire flower garden and proudly presented Mr. Henry with the prize she'd been seeking: an old cow bone. She had been named after the Hoover vacuum cleaner, because she'd sucked up a large pepperoni pizza with extra cheese when she was a mere seven weeks old.

"All right," said Mr. Henry, rubbing his hands together in eager anticipation. "Let's get going. Will the team captains please come up front?"

Five students, including Karen, went to the front of the room.

"Trash captain?"

Julie Horwitz stepped forward.

"All trash collectors, raise your hands."

The four members of Julie's team raised their hands. Mr. Henry ran through each team to make sure everyone knew what to do.

There was a team in charge of removing fallen leaves and twigs. The debris would be carried to the school grounds, where the class, as another project, was going to create a compost pile.

There was a team to prepare a new flower bed along the cemetery fence, and another to plant and water the flowers. The biggest team was Karen's. Allie was on it, along with Pam, Dub, Joey Fratto, and Brad Lewis. They were in charge of clearing dirt and over-growth from the graves, and cleaning and straightening the headstones.

"Okay," said Mr. Henry. "Let's go. And remember how we talked about acting respectful when you're in the cemetery."

"We don't want to stir up any ghosts," said Dub.

Allie shivered as two light but chilly hands touched her shoulders. She turned quickly to see who had come sneaking up behind her. There was no one there. She glanced around to see if anyone else appeared to have seen or felt anything unusual. But her teammates were busily gathering their tools.

Something very strange was happening, Allie thought. And, for some reason, it was happening to *her*.

Eight

Situated as it was on the ridge above Fossil Glen, the cemetery was a peaceful and scenic spot. When they were all inside the old wrought-iron fence that surrounded the graveyard, Mr. Henry told the team members to decide among themselves how to get the work done. Allie's team stood looking at one another.

"Boys in one group, girls in another," announced Brad. "Come on, guys. We'll start on this end."

"All right," said Dub agreeably.

"Okay," said Allie.

"Wait," Karen said. "Pam and I decided we want to be partners, right, Pam?"

"Right," said Pam.

"So what's the problem?" asked Joey. "You guys and Allie are one group, we're the other. Bet *we* get twice as much work done!" he challenged with a wicked grin.

"The problem," Karen said slowly, as if Joey were some kind of moron, "is that Pam and I want to work alone. Just the two of us. We think it will be better that way. Don't we, Pam?"

Pam nodded.

Allie looked from Karen to Pam. Karen gazed back with a pitying smile. Pam's eyes darted everywhere except toward Allie. The week before, when the teams were first formed, the three girls had talked about what fun it would be to work together.

Joey looked bewildered. Allie could feel her face turning bright red with humiliation. She looked down at the ground, wishing she could disappear.

"Oh, I get it," said Dub with a dangerous smile. "You two don't want to give the rest of us your disease. Well, thanks a lot for sparing us. That's very thoughtful of you."

"Dub Whitwell, that's not what I meant and you know it," said Karen indignantly.

Dub ignored her. "Fine. We'll have three groups of two instead," he said, directing his remarks to Brad and Joey. "You guys be partners. Come on, Al. Let's us get started over at the far end."

Karen smiled sweetly at Allie with her chin in the air, and turned to Pam. "So, did you watch *Teen Twins* last night?" she asked.

"Yeah," answered Pam.

"Wasn't it great when that geek Susan went up to Brian and said, 'I got your note'? The look on his face was so funny."

The girls' voices rose in peals of laughter as they walked away.

Allie stood where she was, feeling as if she'd been punched in the stomach. Dub looked at her and shrugged. "Looks like you're stuck with me," he said.

"Not stuck, dummy," she said, trying to smile back at him.

They began walking to the far wall of the graveyard. "What's up with Queen Karen and her faithful companion, Whatever-You-Say-Karen?" Dub asked.

"I don't know," Allie answered miserably. "I guess they're mad at me."

"How come?"

Allie told him what Karen had said on the phone.

"Oh," said Dub, frowning. "She was just letting you know 'as a friend,' eh? Well," he added cheerfully, "you know what they say—with friends like those two, who needs enemies?"

"Dub!" Allie protested. "We *are* friends. It's just a— misunderstanding. I haven't had a chance to explain, that's all." Almost to herself, she added, "And I even watched *Teen Twins* last night."

"Twin Airheads?" Dub looked at Allie unbelievingly. "Tell me you don't watch that junk." Putting on a falsetto voice, he imitated one of the twins: "Oh, my

hair got mussed! Whatever shall I do? My life is ruined!"
He pretended to sob hysterically, then peeked at Allie.

She couldn't help laughing. "I only watched five
minutes," she said. "It did seem pretty stupid. But
Karen and Pam like it a lot. Maybe it takes a while to
get into it."

Dub gave Allie a look she couldn't quite fathom.
She didn't want to talk about Karen and Pam with
Dub, so she went to work on the first gravestone in the
row along the fence. The stone lay flat on the ground.
Allie swept the leaves away and read aloud, "Walter
Oswald Emmons, Beloved husband."

"Look," said Dub. "Here's his wife, Irma, right next
to him."

"That's nice, the way they're buried side by side,
don't you think?" asked Allie as she scraped away the
moss and grass that had grown over the stone.

"I guess so," said Dub. "I mean, if you have to be
here."

They moved down the row, clearing off each headstone, trying their best to straighten those that had
heaved in the winter frost, removing trash and forgotten offerings of dead flowers and tattered flags.

Allie heard Dub hoot with laughter. "Listen to this,"
he called. " 'Here lies Orvin Killigrew, a wretched,
poor, and lowly worm.' "

"No way!" said Allie. She walked over to read the
headstone herself.

"How would you like that on your gravestone?" Dub asked.

"Geez," said Allie, with a giggle. "Poor guy."

They moved on to the next tombstone and began brushing the leaves away. It was fun working with Dub. The sun felt warm on her shoulders and she was enjoying the glimpses that the headstone carvings offered into the lives of those long-gone people.

She walked over to a small stone that stood upright in the ground. While most of the graves sat in family groupings, this one was off by itself, spaced farther away from the others than was usual. And while many of the others were decorated with angels or flowers or comforting words, this one appeared stark and bare by comparison. Drawing closer, Allie felt a chill again, despite the sun.

She read the simple inscription: "Lucy Stiles, 1983–1994." Doing some quick subtraction in her head, she gasped. "Dub, look! This girl was only eleven when she died. *Our age.*"

Dub came over to see, and it was then that the significance of the name struck Allie. "Lucy Stiles, Dub! *Stiles.*" To emphasize her meaning, she pointed across the field to the deserted house.

"Hmmm," said Dub, examining the carved dates. "1994. That's only four years ago."

Figuring quickly, Allie said, "When we were in second grade. I wonder how she died."

Dub assumed the deep voice and macho stance of a TV cop. "I'm afraid we suspect foul play, ma'am," he said.

Allie began to laugh. She stopped abruptly at the sound of a low voice, not quite a whisper.

"Did you hear that?" she asked Dub.

"What?"

"That voice."

"You mean Joey? How can you miss him? It's like his mouth is hooked up to speakers."

"No, not Joey. It was *the voice*. It sounded as if somebody was right *here.*"

Dub made an exaggerated show of looking all around, over his shoulder, behind his back, behind Allie's back. "Ah, yes," he agreed. "I see who you mean. It's Orvin Killigrew, the poor, wretched worm, standing right behind you."

"Dub, I'm serious. I heard the voice again. And this morning, in the classroom, I felt cold hands on my shoulders." She stopped, and her hand flew to her mouth. "Right after you said something about ghosts." She looked at Dub, wide-eyed.

"Al," he said. "You're sounding kind of whacked, if you don't mind my saying so."

"Dub, this is so weird."

"You got that right," said Dub.

"And there's something else," said Allie. "You know my journal?"

"That book you told me about? Did you use it?"

"Yes. And remember I looked through it and told you all the pages were blank?"

Dub nodded.

"Well, last night I found writing in it."

"So you missed it when you looked," Dub said matter-of-factly.

Allie tried to keep the impatience out of her voice as she said, "I'm *sure* I didn't. The page was blank when I left the room, I know it was. I closed the book, went to get a pen, and when I came back it was open to the first page, and—there it was."

"What?"

"Writing. Just the words, 'I am,' and then the letter 'L.' Capital L. Like the beginning of a name. Only it sort of broke off, as if the person who wrote it had stopped suddenly."

"Michael?" Dub suggested.

Allie shook her head. "He wasn't around. I looked. Besides, he can't write, especially in cursive. He's only four."

There was a moment of silence, during which Dub appeared to be deep in thought. "So who's 'L'?" he asked.

"I don't know," answered Allie quietly.

"Have you told anybody else about this?" asked Dub.

"My parents," said Allie. "And they didn't believe

me. They said the writing had to have been there all along and that the rest of it was just my imagination running away with me." She sighed in exasperation. "So I wrote about it in my journal last night."

"You told Mr. Henry you were hearing voices?" asked Dub.

"I couldn't think of anything else to write about."

"You'd better hope he keeps his promise not to show anyone," said Dub. "Like the little men in white coats."

"Very funny," said Allie. "Dub, you don't think I'm making this up, do you?"

"No," said Dub. "Maybe Karen can't tell when you're fooling around and when you're serious, but I can."

"And I'm not crazy," she declared.

Dub's face gathered in a sarcastic leer, as if he was about to crack a joke. Then he must have caught the worried look on Allie's face. "No way," he said.

Allie felt relieved. She glanced again at the stone near their feet. " 'L' could stand for Lucy."

"Except for one small problem," said Dub.

"What?"

"Duh, Al. She's *dead*, remember?"

Allie giggled nervously. "That *would* be a problem."

Nine

The sound of the twelve o'clock whistle carried from the fire station to the cemetery. The class gathered their bag lunches and walked over to the glen to picnic by the creek. When Allie saw Karen and Pam sitting close together and sharing their lunches, she sat down near Mr. Henry. Dub joined her.

"Joey, you remembered your lunch?" Mr. Henry asked with a grin.

"When it comes to food," said Joey, "I don't forget."

From their flat, sunny picnic spot at the edge of the meadow, they could look down into the steep ravine that formed Fossil Glen. The silver stream of water rushed by, tumbling around corners and over rocks and fallen trees.

Allie nibbled on her peanut-butter-and-jelly sandwich, trying to concentrate on the flowing stream and the warmth of the sun on her back, instead of on Karen and Pam, who were looking her way and whispering. About half a mile downstream, Allie knew, the waters of Fossil Creek emptied into the wide, deep bowl of Seneca Lake.

Swollen with the spring rains, the creek seemed to be hurrying recklessly toward the lake. Later on, when summer came, the stream would slow down and warm up. It was as if it suddenly realized it didn't want to lose itself in the large, cold waters of the lake, Allie thought, and she smiled to herself.

Dub reached over and took a handful of potato chips from Allie's bag. "The stream looks so small from up here," he said.

"It sure does," Mr. Henry agreed. "It's hard to believe that little creek carved out this entire glen. These cliffs are over two hundred feet high."

"Wait a second," said Julie. "Do you mean the creek used to be up here, where we are?"

"That's right," said Mr. Henry. "Slowly, slowly, it cut its way down through the dirt and rock to form the glen."

"Wow. It must have taken a long time."

"Where did all the fossils come from?" asked Joey.

"They're from the time when this whole area was under a warm, tropical ocean," Mr. Henry told them.

"And then, millions of years later, it was covered by glaciers, right?" said Dub.

"Right," said Mr. Henry.

"I don't believe it," declared Karen.

"It's true," said Mr. Henry. "Where we're sitting right now used to be the bottom of the sea." Everyone was quiet for a minute, trying to picture it.

"That's awesome," said Joey.

"We could spend the rest of the year just studying the history and ecology of the glen," said Mr. Henry. "After all, here it is, right in our own back yard. And, as you're all noticing, it's really a very interesting place."

"And pretty," said Julie.

To her surprise, Allie heard her own voice add, "But it's haunted."

A shiver seized her, and she dropped her bag of chips. Fumbling to stuff the chips back in the bag, she heard the same faint whisper she had described to Dub. She felt his eyes on her and glanced up. He looked worried.

"What do you mean, haunted?" asked Karen scornfully.

"I—I don't—" Allie shrugged and looked down at her lap, embarrassed. She didn't know why she'd said that.

"Oh, I get it," said Dub. "It's haunted by the ghosts of the Indians who used to live here. The Senecas."

Allie knew Dub was trying to help her out. Opening her mouth to answer, she heard the whisper again, and the back of her neck felt prickly and cold. Again, to her surprise, she heard her own voice speak. "No," it said. "Someone else."

Karen made a disgusted face. "Here we go," she muttered, but softly, so Mr. Henry wouldn't hear. "This ought to be good."

Dub glared angrily at Karen. Mr. Henry, unaware of the tension, laughed. "Allie must be thinking of the spirits of all those little critters who died and became fossilized in these cliffs."

Allie forced herself to smile and nod, unable to open her mouth again for fear of what might come out.

"Those are two subjects we might pursue," Mr. Henry continued. "The creatures and the native people who lived here before us. And, speaking of people who lived before us, I guess we'd better get back to the cemetery and go to work."

Everyone rose, picked up the picnic clutter, and started walking back to the cemetery. Allie could feel Dub eyeing her warily.

"Don't ask me what happened," she said, "because I don't know. I didn't mean to say anything. It was as if someone else was talking, not me."

Dub was quiet.

"Say something," Allie pleaded. "You think I'm a nut case, don't you?"

"No," said Dub slowly. "But I think we'd better figure out what the heck is going on."

Allie was relieved to hear Dub say "we."

"What are you doing after school?" Dub asked.

Allie thought for a minute. Then she remembered. "I'm supposed to go down to Mom's shop to look at a desk."

"Oh," said Dub, "okay."

"Why?"

"I thought maybe you could come over and we could fool around on the computer. Maybe do some searches."

Allie was puzzled. "Searches? For what?"

Dub shrugged. "I don't know. Stuff about ghosts."

Allie stared at him. "Ghosts? Dub, you don't really think—" She stopped. She could see that Dub was serious. And, the truth was, it was exactly what she'd been thinking, but she'd been afraid to say it out loud. She hadn't even wanted to think about the possibility . . .

Ghosts.

For as long as she could remember, she'd been hoping for something really exciting to happen. She'd believed in the unbelievable, expected the unexpected. She'd *wanted* it to be true that there was more to life than the everyday world people saw. But now that something totally inexplicable seemed to be happening, and happening to her, she felt partly thrilled and partly afraid.

"I know," said Allie. "Come with me to the shop. It won't take long to look at a desk. Then we can go to your house."

"Okay," agreed Dub.

They reached the cemetery and began working where they had left off. Soon they met the other members of the team near the middle. When they had straightened and cleaned the last headstone, they all stood together and stretched their tired backs. Most of the other teams were finishing up, too, and were looking around at the results of their work.

"Hey, this place looks great," said Brad.

Mr. Henry joined them. "It sure does." He called the rest of the class over and said, "The buses will be at school soon, so we need to get back to the room quickly to get ready for dismissal."

He looked around again and smiled. "You should all feel proud of what you accomplished here today. I've been thinking: what if we turned Earth Day into Earth Week or even Earth Month? We still have our composting project to do, and we seem to have lots and lots of questions about Fossil Creek and Fossil Glen."

The kids nodded enthusiastically.

"Of course," said Mr. Henry with a smile, "that means we'll have to come back here for lots of field trips. Maybe you'd rather stay in the classroom all spring?"

"No way!"

"Field trips, all right!"

Somebody cheered, and Joey gave an ear-splitting whistle of approval.

Karen raised her hand. "Do we have any homework tonight?"

"No homework."

"Yes!"

"Excellent!"

"But I'll probably be up half the night doing mine," added Mr. Henry.

The class looked at him quizzically.

"I'll be reading your journals," he said. "And knowing you all, I'm sure I have a fascinating evening ahead of me."

Dub and Allie exchanged a glance. "Little does he know," said Dub with a mischievous grin.

Ten

"Hi, Mom," Allie called as she and Dub walked through the door of Mrs. Nichols's shop.

"Hi, Al. Back here," a muffled voice replied.

Allie and Dub walked through the main part of the store, past tastefully arranged groupings of furniture, paintings, china, glassware, quilts, and books to a small room that seemed to be overflowing with clutter. Papers, folders, empty packing boxes, crumpled newspapers, and an odd assortment of antiques and framed pictures were piled haphazardly on every available surface.

Mrs. Nichols was bending over a carton, poking through the contents. She looked up, brushing her hair from her face, leaving a streak of dirt across her forehead. She looked hot and sweaty, and her clothing was covered with dust. "Hi, you two."

"Gee, Mom," said Allie, looking around, "if my room looked like this, you'd have a fit."

"It *is* a mess, isn't it?" said Mrs. Nichols cheerfully. "It's all this new stock I've gotten in the past two days. I'm trying to unpack, clean, and price everything, and, wouldn't you know, *customers* keep coming in and distracting me!"

She turned to Dub. "You didn't know how glamorous this job was, did you?"

Dub laughed. "We could help," he said.

"That's nice of you, Dub. And I'd take you up on it, except that right now everything is so disorganized I wouldn't know where to tell you to start."

"Where'd you get all this stuff, Mom?" Allie asked.

"I told you about the man in the van, didn't I?"

"Oh, yeah."

"Remember this morning when we passed the Stiles house and I said I thought I recognized the van in the driveway? Well, I was right. It was the same one. That's where all these new items came from."

Allie lifted her eyebrows. "All this is from the Stiles house?"

"Yes."

"Is someone new moving in?" Dub asked.

"I don't know. But I'd certainly be glad to see someone living in that beautiful old house. It's a shame for it to stand vacant like that." Mrs. Nichols's face brightened as she remembered something. "You came to see the desk, didn't you? Come on. It's right out here."

Allie and Dub followed Mrs. Nichols to the front of the shop. "What do you think?"

By the window were an old-fashioned wooden desk and a matching chair. The desk had a high back with lots of little drawers and pigeonholes. Allie lifted the lid of the slanted writing surface. Inside were more drawers and cubbyholes. Larger drawers on both sides reached to the floor.

The wood seemed to glow in the warm afternoon light that streamed through the window. Allie breathed deeply, catching the scent of lemon polish. "It's so beautiful," she said, rubbing her hand along the polished surface. Turning to her mother, she asked, "May I really have it?"

Mrs. Nichols nodded. "If you like it, it's yours."

"I love it," said Allie.

"Tell you what," said Mrs. Nichols. "Why don't you two remove all the drawers to make it lighter. Then the three of us should have no problem carrying it. I'll bring the car around to the front door, and we'll see if we can fit it in."

Working together, they managed to wrestle the desk into the back seat of the car, and the drawers and the chair into the trunk.

"There," said Mrs. Nichols. "But there's no room for you two now."

"That's okay," said Allie. "We were thinking about going to Dub's to look up some stuff on his computer, anyway."

"All right. But be home by six for dinner."

"Okay. After dinner, can we put the desk in my room?"

"Of course."

"Bye, Mrs. Nichols," said Dub.

"Nice to see you, Dub."

"Thanks, Mom."

"Bye, sweetie."

As she and Dub walked up the main street of town toward Dub's house, Allie thought how strange it was that her new desk came from the Stiles house, and her mind flashed on the image of Lucy Stiles's lonely grave.

When they arrived at Dub's house, he opened the door with a key he wore around his neck. No one was home. Dub's mother traveled a lot for her job with a computer company, and his father was still at work. It was because of his mother's job that Dub always had the most up-to-the-minute computer and programs.

They got a package of cookies and some milk and sat side by side in front of the computer. Dub turned it on. While it clicked and whirred, he said, "Let's try typing in the key word 'ghost' and see what we get."

"Okay," said Allie. She watched, fascinated, as Dub

used the mouse and keyboard to skip from screen to screen. Mumbling to himself, he said, "Space ghost, no. Ghost towns, no. Chinese hopping ghosts . . ."

"That sounds interesting," said Allie.

"I know, but we can't get distracted. It's not really what we're looking for," said Dub, continuing to scroll through the list of ghost-related topics.

"What *are* we looking for?" asked Allie.

"Here we go! Ghost stories are us . . . Ghosts around the world . . . True ghost stories . . . Let's try that." He clicked the mouse on the third entry.

Allie read aloud, quickly jumping from one paragraph to another: " 'True ghost stories . . . gathered from over two hundred people and twenty countries . . . Brief text of each story . . . followed by an analysis of common elements . . .' Okay, keep going."

Allie and Dub scanned screen after screen of tales told by people who claimed to have been visited by ghosts. Amid the fantastic tales were repeated references to both whispered and written messages from the ghost. Often, people told of feeling shivers or chills in its presence. Ghosts appeared to people in many different ways, and their powers were quite varied. Sometimes they caused events, sometimes they encouraged a living person to make things happen.

At last, Allie and Dub reached the end of the stories.

"Wow," said Dub. "Makes you wonder, doesn't it?"

Allie shifted uneasily in her chair. "Let's see what it

says here at the end." She continued reading aloud: " 'Many of the stories suggest that the strength and ability of a ghost are related to the age and power of the person at the time of his or her death. The ghost of an infant, therefore, is often said to be weak and ineffectual, perhaps making its presence known only by the faint sound of its cries. The ghost of a forty-year-old woman, on the other hand, may be able to make itself known to humans in many different ways in order to influence earthly events.' "

Allie looked at Dub. "Strange, huh? Now listen to this: 'In almost every case, the ghost is an unwilling spirit who was treated unfairly in life and who can find no rest until the wrongs against him or her are redressed.

" 'Some ghosts seek revenge, others seek justice. Some appear to the person who wronged them; others choose a person, often a stranger, whom they believe can make things right again. Then, and only then, can the spirit be at peace and leave the human world behind. This theme is the most common feature of all human encounters with ghosts, regardless of the country or culture of origin.' "

Allie sighed. "Well, if I'm going crazy, at least I'm not alone. Actually, reading all these other people's stories makes me feel *less* crazy. It makes me think we're on the right track. But you know what I wonder most of all?"

"Who the ghost—if it is a ghost—is?"

"Yes, that. But, even more . . ." She paused. "Why did it pick *me*?"

Dub thought for a moment. "Good question."

Allie glanced up at the clock on the wall. "Oh! It's after six. I'd better call Mom and tell her I'm on my way."

"Go ahead," Dub said. "The computer's on a separate line."

She picked up the phone and dialed, while Dub kept clicking from one screen to another. "Dad? It's me. Dub and I were working on the computer and lost track of the time. Yeah. I'm leaving right now. Okay. Bye."

To Dub she said, "I've got to go. See you tomorrow."

But Dub was deep in cyberspace again. "Okay, Al," he said, without taking his eyes from the screen. "See you later."

Allie walked home, feeling excited, but jittery. Every few moments she looked back over her shoulder, half expecting to see or hear something. It appeared, at least so far, that the ghost meant her no harm. Still, she couldn't help feeling thankful that nightfall was at least an hour away.

Eleven

After dinner, Allie and her parents unloaded the desk from the car, carried it upstairs to her room, and arranged it against the wall in place of the old plywood-and-block table.

Mrs. Nichols squinted critically at the desk, shifted it slightly to the right, then to the left. Finally, she said, "It looks nice right there, don't you think?"

"It's perfect," said Allie.

Michael appeared at the door, holding a tablet and a box of crayons. "Can I color at your new desk, Allie?" he asked.

Allie smiled when she saw his serious expression. "You have some important work to do?" she asked.

Michael nodded.

"Okay. Come here," said Allie. She pulled out the chair for him, and Michael sat down and opened his crayon box.

"Don't you have any homework, now that you have an official desk to do it on?" asked her father.

"Nope," said Allie happily. "We don't even have to write in our journals tonight. Mr. Henry collected them today. He's probably reading them right now."

Allie glanced up and caught a look passing between her parents. They sat down, Mr. Nichols in the chair opposite Allie's, Mrs. Nichols on the bed. Michael, seated in Allie's new chair, was concentrating on his paper.

"If you don't have any homework, honey," her mother said gently, "would you like to talk about what happened with Karen and Pam?"

Allie sighed. "Not really," she said.

"It's not always easy for three people to be friends," said Mrs. Nichols. "Someone usually ends up feeling left out."

"Yeah," said Allie. "Like me."

"Your mother said they called you a liar," said her father. "What was that all about?"

Allie groaned inwardly. She was going to have to go through the whole thing all over again. Her parents were both looking at her with earnest, serious expressions. She knew they only wanted to help, but she really didn't feel like talking about it.

"We were talking at lunch about a teacher at school, Mr. Pinkney, and about Ms. Gillespie and Mrs. Hobbs—she's this really crabby cafeteria lady—and trying to figure out how they ended up working at our school. I mean, that's what I thought we were doing: just fooling around and making up theories," she explained as patiently as she could.

Her parents sat listening, their eyebrows lifted with interest and concern, waiting for her to say more. When she didn't, her father said, "So these theories of yours about Ms. Gillespie and the others—were they true?"

"I don't know," said Allie, trying not to sound as exasperated as she felt. "Probably not. That's what I'm trying to tell you: we were just speculating. And I was being kind of silly, on purpose. Trying to imagine, for example, what a guy like Mr. Pinkney is doing teaching *gym*."

Mr. and Mrs. Nichols met with Mr. Pinkney each year at Open House Night at school. Allie's father was trying unsuccessfully to hide a grin. "I can see how you might wonder," he said.

"So I was trying to think of possible reasons," Allie went on. "I like to try and figure people out."

"But you were just guessing," said her mother.

"Well, yeah," answered Allie. "Of course."

"And sometimes your theories are so convincing that you believe they're real?" her mother probed.

Allie squirmed uncomfortably. "No. But some things I just *know*. The basic facts are obvious to anybody with eyes."

"You've always been mighty observant, Allie-Cat," her father said with a smile.

"Just so you keep the facts separate from the theories," said her mother.

"I know the difference, Mom," said Allie.

"Maybe you need to explain it to Karen and Pam," said her mother.

"Maybe," said Allie doubtfully. "I'll try." It sounded like a good idea. But how did you explain something to people who didn't even want to talk to you?

Her parents left the room, her father patting her shoulder reassuringly, her mother quickly kissing her cheek. Allie sat where she was and sighed, feeling her excitement over the new desk slowly leaking away. She looked at Michael, who was sitting on his knees on the desk chair, leaning over his coloring.

He carefully folded his paper in half and handed it to Allie. "Here," he said. "I made it for you."

Allie opened the page and saw that Michael had drawn two figures. One was obviously a girl, with straight brown hair like Allie's and a big red smile. The other was a boy wearing Michael's favorite X-Man shirt. The two figures were about the same size and seemed to be holding hands.

"That's you," said Michael, pointing to the paper.

"And that's me. Except it's when I'm grown up and I'm eleven, too."

Allie smiled. She didn't tell Michael that when he was eleven years old, she would be eighteen, hard as that was to imagine.

Michael continued his explanation of the picture. "See? We're friends." He looked at Allie very seriously. "And I never, ever call you a liar."

Allie felt tears spring to her eyes. She grabbed Michael in a fierce bear hug so he wouldn't think it was his picture that had made her sad.

"Thanks, Mikey," she whispered in his ear. She breathed in his little-boy smell, a combination of No More Tears shampoo and some peanut butter that she saw was stuck in his hair. "I love it. It's going right here," she said, and taped the picture on the wall over her desk.

Mr. Nichols put his head in the door to tell Michael it was time to get ready for bed, and Allie sat down at the desk to think. It was clear that she saw and heard things that others didn't. Like the face of a girl with curly black hair. Like the voice of a girl saying, "Help me."

Her parents tried to understand, but they didn't really get it. How could she tell them now that she was pretty sure she was being visited by a ghost?

Twelve

Later that night Allie lay on her back in bed, still and helpless, as someone's hands tightened menacingly around her neck. Slowly and with great strength, the hands closed tighter and tighter. Allie felt her lungs about to burst in her chest. Finally, in a frenzy, she managed to struggle free. She had a brief moment of relief before, gasping for air, she felt herself falling, falling, falling from a great height.

She fell for a long, long time, it seemed, and as she fell, a peculiar thing happened. At some point, it was no longer she who was plunging through the air, but someone else. Allie was standing above, watching another girl drop slowly from a high precipice. Black curly hair blew about in a tangled mass, then fell away to reveal the girl's face. Her eyes were wide and filled with fear—and something else, a terrible anger.

Allie was vaguely aware of a threatening presence somewhere near her, but she couldn't pull her eyes away from the awful, mesmerizing figure of the tumbling girl, who was about to hit the ground.

Allie's hands flew to cover her eyes and she awakened with a cry, her nightgown soaked in sweat, her heart pounding wildly. She tried to rise, but she was tangled in the covers and had to fight her way free. With a gasp, she threw the blanket to the floor and sat up on the edge of the bed. She shuddered as the cool breeze from the window hit her damp skin.

Struggling through the hazy layers of sleep, she realized that she'd been dreaming. She reached to touch her throat, and the nightmare came rushing back. She remembered the feeling of hands closing around her neck, the desperate struggle for breath, the sickening sensation of falling. Allie moaned. "What a horrible dream." She rubbed her eyes. It had seemed so real. The girl herself had seemed real.

It was the same face that had appeared to her the day her journal arrived in the mailbox.

Who was she?

Allie got up and headed down the hall to the bathroom. She heard the murmur of her parents' voices as she passed their bedroom. On her way back to bed, she heard her own name and stopped to listen.

"—think she should see someone about it?" said her mother.

"What do you mean, someone?" said her father. "Like who?"

"Like a counselor."

"A psychiatrist?"

"Or a psychologist."

"Do you think it would help?"

"I don't know. I don't even know if it's really a problem. She's always had an active imagination. It's not something I want to discourage, exactly. It's just that I hate to see her lose friends over it."

"So do I. And I worry sometimes that she doesn't know the difference between what's real and what isn't. This thing about the words appearing in her journal . . ."

"I know. It's peculiar, to say the least."

There was silence for a minute. Allie waited expectantly.

Her father spoke again. "Let's give it a while. She's really such a levelheaded kid. And she seems okay except for this thing with Karen and Pam."

"You know, sixth-grade girls can be cruel to one another for no good reason," Mrs. Nichols said thoughtfully.

"Maybe that's what's going on," said Mr. Nichols.

"She gets along fine with Dub."

"And her teacher seems quite fond of her. Her grades are good."

"You're right," said Allie's mother. "I'm probably worrying too much, making a mountain out of a molehill." There was a long silence, during which Allie anxiously held her breath. Finally, her mother said, "Let's keep a careful eye on her for a while, though, shall we?"

"Good idea."

Quietly, Allie let out a sigh of relief. Her parents weren't going to make a federal case out of the situation—at least for the moment. She tiptoed back to bed, vowing not to give her parents any further reason to worry about her.

Thirteen

At school the next day, Mr. Henry handed back the students' journals. The room grew quiet as everyone studied Mr. Henry's comments. Eagerly, Allie read:

Nice job, Allie. This story is very intriguing. I like the way you began with the mysterious message: "I am L." Right away, I was curious to read more. This shows good imagination! I can't wait to see what will happen next.

Allie smiled. Mr. Henry had liked her journal entry. He had praised her imagination! Of course, she thought, he doesn't know I'm writing about things that really happened. He thinks I'm making up a story. But he found it "intriguing." Allie thought that was a good word to describe what was going on.

She raised her head as Mr. Henry began to speak again. "I noticed that some of you had a little trouble getting started," he said. "I'm hoping that writing in your journals will come to be a pleasure, not a chore. I really meant it when I said you may write about anything you like. You're not writing to please me but to stretch your imaginations and to talk to yourselves about the things that are going on in your lives.

"Some of you wrote about private thoughts and problems, which is fine. Others of you wrote very unusual pieces." He looked at Allie. "Allie, how would you feel about reading your entry out loud? You don't have to say yes. I was just thinking that your story would be a good example of an entry that was a little different."

Allie hesitated. Mr. Henry's request had caught her by surprise. She felt torn between pride and embarrassment.

"Come on, Allie," said Joey. "Let's hear it."

"Yeah, Allie. Read," other voices urged.

"You don't have to if you don't want to," Mr. Henry repeated.

"It's okay," said Allie. She looked around at her classmates. Most of them were regarding her with great interest. Dub was grinning encouragingly. She glanced toward Karen and was immediately sorry. Karen's arms were folded across her chest and she mouthed the words, "Teacher's pet."

Allie looked away and, reluctantly, began to read.

" 'I am L.' The words appeared, mysteriously, on the opening page of my journal. I sat down to write and there they were. But that is not the beginning of the story."

Allie continued reading until she came to the end: " 'Who is L? I plan to find out.' "

There was a brief silence before the class broke into spontaneous applause. All except for Pam, who was looking at Karen, and Karen, who was staring off into space with a bored expression on her face.

"Cool story, Al," said Brad.

Other voices echoed, "Yeah."

"What's going to happen next?" asked Trisha.

"Who cares," Allie heard Karen mutter.

"I don't know," said Allie. Boy, was that the truth!

Mr. Henry was beaming at her. "Thanks, Allie. I enjoyed it even more the second time. After hearing that example of imaginative writing, I hope all of you will cut loose in your journals and express yourselves as freely as you like.

"But now please put your journals away and let's head down to the library," Mr. Henry said. "I talked with Mrs. Foster about your interest in Fossil Glen and she had a terrific idea. She suggested that we alternate field-study trips to the glen with research trips to the library. She's all set to help you find answers to the questions we raised yesterday. So get your pencils and notebooks and let's go."

As they walked through the hall to the library, Mr.

Henry fell into step beside Allie. "I hope I didn't put you on the spot, Allie," he said. "I really wanted the rest of the class to hear your work."

Allie shook her head. "It's okay," she said. "I didn't mind." They walked a few steps in silence. Then Allie said, "Mr. Henry?"

"Yes?"

"Do you think anything like that could really happen?"

"Do you mean something like what happened in your story?" asked Mr. Henry.

"Yes."

Mr. Henry looked into Allie's face for a moment before answering carefully. "I think this, Allie: The world is a very complex, interesting place. Sometimes things happen that we don't understand. It doesn't mean there isn't an explanation. We simply haven't found it yet."

Allie thought about that. It made sense.

"Why do you ask?" said Mr. Henry. He wasn't making fun of her; he looked serious, as if he really wanted to know.

For a second she thought about confiding in Mr. Henry. Then she remembered her parents' conversation the evening before. If they talked to Mr. Henry . . .

No, she'd better keep quiet. For now. They were approaching the library door, anyway. "Oh, I don't know," she answered. "I just wondered."

"Well, keep wondering," said Mr. Henry with a smile. "That's how we learn."

They walked into the library. As usual, it was a busy place, filled with children choosing books, watching filmstrips, listening to cassettes, working on projects, and clicking away on the computers. Mrs. Foster, the librarian, was everywhere at once, it seemed, answering questions and offering advice on how to find things. There was a table piled high with materials she had gathered for Allie's class.

"Mr. Henry tells me you want to know *everything,*" she said with a smile. "So I've pulled out information on fossils, lake and stream ecology, and the Seneca Indians, for starters. There's a pile of newspapers, too, containing articles about the recent and not so recent history of the glen. Come to me if you have any questions, and I'll be happy to help you."

After looking through the stacks of materials, the students scattered to tables to work. Mr. Henry had told them each to think of one question about Fossil Glen and try to find the answer. That afternoon, they would share what they had learned.

Allie headed straight for the information Mrs. Foster had gathered about fossils. She was about to reach for a book called *Secrets in Stone,* when she heard the voice inside her head.

"Look at the newspapers," it said.

Allie froze.

"*The newspapers,*" repeated the voice.

Forcing herself to act natural, Allie walked toward the table that held a stack of old editions of the local paper, *The Seneca Times*. She riffled through the pile. A photograph of a young girl with dark curly hair caught her eye.

It was the girl from her nightmare, the girl whose face had appeared to her in the kitchen!

Fourteen

The headline blared in large black letters: RESCUE WORKERS SEARCH FOSSIL GLEN FOR MISSING GIRL. The paper was dated Thursday, May 19, 1994. Allie began to read.

> The search for Lucy Stiles continues.

Lucy Stiles! Allie's mind flew to the small, lonely grave she and Dub had found in the cemetery. With a mixture of curiosity and dread, she continued reading.

> Village and state police are asking for the public's help in locating an eleven-year-old girl who was last seen by her mother at about 5:30 Wednesday night.

Rebecca A. Stiles, the girl's mother, reported to police that she became worried when it grew dark and her daughter had not returned from fossil hunting in Fossil Glen. Searching the glen, Mrs. Stiles found a blue sweatshirt belonging to her daughter on the cliff above the third falls, along with a small pile of fossils. When it began to grow dark, Mrs. Stiles left the glen to call for help.

Police, fire and rescue workers, and volunteers searched through the night. Officials speculate that Lucy lost her footing on the steep, rocky precipice and fell.

"There was a drizzly rain last night, and that made the cliff real slick," said Police Chief Ron Webster. "If she fell onto the rocks, we'd have found her. We figure she must have fallen into the creek and gotten washed downstream. That creek's running pretty good, so we've been searching along the banks, hoping she pulled herself out."

So far, searches have found no further sign of the girl. Tomorrow, officials are planning to drag the lake bottom near the mouth of the creek. Divers will also join the search.

"We're still hoping to find her alive," said Chief Webster. But he admitted to reporters that that possibility was becoming increasingly remote.

The missing girl is described as being 4′ 6″ tall, with blue eyes and black curly hair. She was last seen wearing jeans, sneakers, a red-and-black-checkered flannel shirt, and the blue sweatshirt that was found at the scene.

Anyone with information about Lucy Stiles or her whereabouts is asked to call the Seneca Village police department.

Allie refolded the paper and grabbed the next day's edition, marked Friday, May 20, 1994. The headline announced: *LUCY STILES STILL MISSING*. The article continued:

Publicly, rescue workers speak hopefully about finding eleven-year-old Lucy Stiles alive. Privately, they express fears that the girl did not survive an apparent fall from the cliffs above Fossil Glen.

Officials searched the creek bed downstream from where the girl's blue sweatshirt and some fossils were found on the cliff, without result. A thorough search of the waters near the mouth of Fossil Creek also failed to produce any sign of the girl, missing since 5:30 p.m. Wednesday.

Seneca Village Police Chief Ron Webster commented, "Every year we warn kids to be careful in that glen, and every year we end up rescuing someone. I sure hate to see a thing like this happen."

He added that "there is no reason to believe this was anything but an accident." Near where Lucy's sweatshirt was left, police found what appeared to be evidence of Lucy's slide off the cliff edge. "We couldn't see clear footprints because of the rain that fell Wednesday night, but there was a long mud slick heading right off the edge of the cliff. I figure that's where she lost her footing," he said.

The search will continue in Seneca Lake. Chief Webster stated grimly, "Except, now, I guess it's a search for the body."

Allie was totally absorbed, reaching for one newspaper after another. The articles became smaller and smaller and less and less hopeful. After five days, the search was abandoned. There was no mention of Lucy Stiles for a week. Then Allie came to an article with the headline: MISSING GIRL BELIEVED DEAD; FUNERAL SERVICES TO BE HELD.

She read that local, county, and state officials had completed their investigation into the death of Lucy Stiles, ultimately declaring it "a tragic and fatal accident."

Lucy's mother, Rebecca Stiles, reluctantly accepted the verdict that Lucy had not survived. Funeral services were to be held at the Presbyterian Church, followed by a burial in Fossil Glen Cemetery.

With amazement she read:

"Seneca Heights School officials were unanimous in their praise for Lucy and their sorrow over her death. Mr. Justin Henry, Lucy's sixth-grade teacher, said, "This has been a nightmare for our whole class. We all loved Lucy, and hoped so much that she'd be back. We will miss her terribly."

Allie looked up, feeling dazed. She caught Dub's eye and motioned for him to come over.

"Look at this," she whispered.

Dub's eyes grew wider as they traveled down the columns of newsprint in one paper after another. When he finished, he let out a low whistle. "Wow. I don't remember hearing anything about this."

"It was four years ago," said Allie. "We were dumb little kids; we didn't know anything."

"I can't believe she had Mr. Henry for a teacher!"

"Let's ask him about it," said Allie. She raised her hand and Mr. Henry came over. Pointing to the news-paper article, she said, "Lucy Stiles was in your class?"

Mr. Henry nodded, and a shadow darkened his usu-ally sunny face. "That was a terrible time," he said. "Sometimes I still can't believe she's dead. Lucy was great; smart and imaginative." He smiled at Allie. "You remind me of her, as a matter of fact."

Allie blushed at the unexpected compliment.

He went on. "I had just begun teaching, so Lucy was one of my very first students. When they said she was dead, I—" He stopped for a moment, swallowed, and shook his head. "It was so sad and senseless, the way it happened. She knew that glen like the back of her hand. She wasn't a careless, reckless kid. That's why I kept hoping it was all a mistake. But after a while there was no point in pretending she was still alive."

Allie and Dub were quiet as Mr. Henry stood by their table, a faraway look on his face. Then Allie asked, "Was she the only kid in the Stiles family?"

"Yes," answered Mr. Henry. "And her father had died a few years before that, so Mrs. Stiles was left all alone."

"Where did she go?" asked Allie.

"To California, I think," said Mr. Henry. "She had family there. I imagine this town was full of painful memories for her."

"Yeah," agreed Allie and Dub solemnly.

"The house just sits there getting more rickety and creepy-looking," Dub said. "I wonder why she never sold it."

"It had been in her husband's family for generations," Mr. Henry answered. "Maybe she couldn't part with it for that reason."

Allie was struck by a sudden perplexing thought. "Hey!" she exclaimed. "The newspaper said Lucy was going to be buried in Fossil Glen Cemetery. Dub and I saw her grave. But if they never found her body . . ." Her voice trailed off in bewilderment. "Who's buried there?"

"It's—what would you call it?—a *symbolic* grave, I guess. Since there was no body, the family buried a box of mementos. The students in my class all wrote letters saying their goodbyes to Lucy. Other people added things, too," said Mr. Henry.

Allie and Dub thought about that for a moment. Mr. Henry glanced around the library and saw that Joey's hand was raised, indicating that he needed help with his research. "Well, you two," he said with a sigh, "I guess you've learned a bitter truth: Fossil Glen is beautiful and interesting and peaceful at times. But it can be plenty dangerous, too."

Dub and Allie looked at each other as Mr. Henry walked away.

"Poor Mr. Henry," said Allie. "It must have been awful for him."

Dub nodded. "Think about Mrs. Stiles," he added.

"What about *Lucy*?" Allie said. "No wonder her spirit can't rest."

"Do you mean what I think you mean?" asked Dub, his eyebrows lifting with excitement.

"Yes!" said Allie. For she was sure now. " 'L' is Lucy. She's the ghost. I saw her falling in a dream last night, just the way it says in the newspaper! Dub, she looks exactly like that picture!"

"Wow!" said Dub. "So what does she want from you?"

"I don't know," said Allie. "But I hope I'll find out soon."

Fifteen

On her way home from school, Allie noticed a FOR SALE sign stuck in the lawn in front of the Stiles house. A bit farther down the street, another sign caught her eye. Large and freshly painted, it stood at the edge of the meadow that led to Fossil Glen:

COMING SOON
GLEN VIEW ACRES
AN EXCLUSIVE COMMUNITY. 50 LUXURY HOMES,
COMPLETE WITH WATER, SEWER, AND ELECTRIC

There was more writing in smaller print, and a phone number to call, but Allie didn't read any further. She was too stunned by the idea of houses filling the lovely meadow that bordered Fossil Glen. She wondered if

Mr. Henry knew about it and, if so, what he would say.

That evening, Allie and her family discussed the news as they sat at the dinner table.

"Is Mrs. Stiles the developer?" asked Mr. Nichols.

"No, the developer is Mr. Curtis's boss. Mrs. Stiles must have sold the property to him, or given her permission for the project," said Mrs. Nichols. "Mr. Curtis came back today, and told me that his boss has been planning to sell the house and develop the land for a long time, but there was some sort of delay. I feel sick about it."

"It'll be gross to have all those houses there," said Allie. "Will it mean we won't be able to go to the glen anymore?"

"I imagine so," said Mr. Nichols. "The Stileses used to let people come and go, but now that the land is being developed, well, who knows? The meadow and the glen itself are both private property."

"So, anyway," Mrs. Nichols went on, "as I was saying, Mr. Curtis came back today."

"Did he have more furniture to sell?" asked Allie's father.

"No," said Mrs. Nichols, looking pointedly at Allie. "He came back to ask if I remembered seeing a red leather-bound book in with the things he'd sold me."

At that, Allie's hand, which had been lifting a forkful of mashed potatoes to her mouth, stopped in midair. Slowly, she lowered it to her plate.

Mr. Nichols looked up with interest. "Allie's journal?" he asked.

"That's what I thought of right away," said Mrs. Nichols. "All he said was that when he was clearing out the house he was supposed to keep his eye out for a red leather-bound book, and it slipped his mind. He said it was very important to his boss to get it back. Mr. Curtis seemed quite distraught, poor man. I got the feeling his boss wasn't at all happy to hear it was missing."

Allie had been quiet throughout this exchange, her thoughts whirling. *Her* red book hadn't been with the things in her mother's shop; it had arrived in the mailbox. But it seemed logical to Allie that there was some connection between her red leather-bound book and the one Mr. Curtis was looking for.

"Did you tell him about my journal?" Allie asked.

"Yes, of course. But when I told him it was empty except for what you'd written in it, he said it couldn't be the book he was looking for."

Allie thought about the words "I am L," which she certainly hadn't written, but she decided that this was not the moment to bring that up.

"There *was* only one book, wasn't there, Allie?" her mother asked.

Allie nodded.

"Well, it's interesting that you're using it as a journal," Mrs. Nichols went on, "because the book he's looking for is a diary, too."

"A diary?" said Allie. "Whose?"

"He didn't say," answered Mrs. Nichols. "He just repeated that it was very important to his employer to get it back."

"So can I keep mine?" Allie asked.

"I guess so," said Mrs. Nichols. A quizzical expression remained on her face. "Although it's rather an odd coincidence, don't you think, that he's looking for a book just like yours?" She shook her head, perplexed.

"It sure is," said Mr. Nichols.

"It sure is," piped up Michael.

"It sure is," Allie repeated with a grin in Michael's direction. "But it doesn't sound as if it's the same book at all," she added, getting up from the table. She asked to be excused and carried her dishes out to the kitchen.

It was time to write her next journal entry.

Sitting at her desk, she opened the book to Mr. Henry's last remarks. With a thrill of excitement, she saw that there was a new entry, written below Mr. Henry's, in the same slanting hand as before. This time, the letters were firmer and steadier.

Look in the desk.

She stared at the words for a moment. Then, with trembling hands, she lifted the lid of the desk. The slanted writing surface gleamed in the light from her reading lamp. The cubbyholes that lined the back were still empty.

She opened the long, thin center drawer. Nothing. One by one, she opened the large drawers on the right side, then the left. Empty.

The words on the page insisted:

Look in the desk.

"All right already," she said aloud. "I'll look again." This time, she used her fingers to feel into every corner, nook, and cranny in the desk. She even tapped the underside of each drawer, hoping to discover a false bottom. But each time she heard the same hollow, empty echo.

There was nothing in the desk. Zip. Zero. Zilch.

Look in the desk.

Sitting back in her chair with a frustrated groan, she pounded her fist on the desktop, right on one of the raised brass hinges. It let out a metallic click.

Carefully, she examined the hinge and saw that her banging had caused a small latch to pop open. The latch was cleverly disguised as part of the hinge. More gently this time, she tapped the same place on the left hinge. Again she heard the metallic click and another latch popped open.

Her heart beating fast now, Allie saw that the hinges at the top of the desk served a cunning dual purpose. They allowed the bottom edge of the slanted desktop to be lifted in the usual manner, revealing the large open area beneath, with its slots and pigeonholes for paper, pens, envelopes, and odds and ends. But when unlatched, the hinges opened again from the top edge: the slanted desktop was made of two layers of wood, with empty space between.

And in that hollow space in the desktop lay a book bound in red leather, a book identical to Allie's journal!

Murmuring "I can't believe it, I can't believe it, I can't believe it," Allie lifted the book out of its hiding place. She closed the desk, set the book down, and opened it.

On the first page, in handwriting that seemed almost as familiar as her own, were the words:

This diary belongs to Lucy Stiles.
PRIVATE – KEEP OUT!
(This means you!!)

Allie began to read.

Sixteen

January 1, 1994

Dear Diary,

You and the other book just like you are the best Christmas presents I got. It was hard to wait until today to begin writing, but I decided that New Year's was the perfect day to start a diary. All your clean white pages and all the days of a brand-new year are ready to be filled. It makes me feel kind of solemn (that's a new vocabulary word) and excited to think about it. Mom says the other book looks just like you, so I didn't even unwrap it. I'm going to save it for <u>next</u> year.

So that's it! thought Allie excitedly. Lucy had been

given two red leather-bound books for Christmas. One became Lucy's diary and the other became—Allie's journal. It came to Allie just as Lucy had left it, still enclosed in the tissue paper that Lucy had never removed.

Is this how you talk to a diary—as if it's a person? Well, that's how I'm going to do it. I think a diary should be like a best friend. I will tell you everything.

First of all, I will tell you about myself. I am eleven. I have curly black hair. I'm too skinny, Mom says, so she's always trying to get me to eat more. I am in sixth grade, and my teacher is Mr. Henry. He's really nice.

I live with my mother. My father died when I was seven. I have two pets, a dog named Bogey and a cat named Crenshaw. I collect fossils and sea glass. That's pieces of broken glass that are smooth from being in the lake for a long time. I think it should be called lake glass, don't you?

Allie smiled as she read this. She, too, collected sea glass, as well as fossils, and had had the same thought about its name.

Mom's calling me to go downstairs now. Her boyfriend is here. She says he's not her boyfriend, but I saw him kiss her last week. It was severely disgusting. Don't ask me how she could stand it. He has brownish-yellow teeth and a teeny little bristly

*mustache and he smells like cigars, which he smokes
until I want to throw up. Well, I've got to go. Bye
till tomorrow.*

January 2, 1994

Dear Diary,
    *First of all, Mom's boyfriend is a <u>BIG JERK</u>. I
can't believe she likes him. She's always telling me
how "fond" he is of me, but it's not true. The thing
is, he acts real nice to me in front of her. It's fake
nice, though. He fools her, but not me. His name is
Raymond Gagney. Gag-Me is more like it!*

Allie laughed out loud at that. No wonder Mr.
Henry had liked Lucy so much, she thought. Lucy was
sassy!

Allie continued to read through the entries for the
month of January and into February. As Lucy confided
her secrets to her diary, Allie felt as if the dead girl
was speaking directly to her. She read about little
things, such as a social-studies report Lucy was writing for Mr. Henry, and big things, too. She learned
that Lucy's father had left Lucy and her mother quite
a bit of money when he died, but that the money didn't
matter to Lucy, who missed her father terribly.

Lucy continued to write unflatteringly about Mr.
Gagney, her mother's boyfriend, whom she referred to
as Gag-Me. Allie recognized in Lucy a kindred spirit.
Like Allie, Lucy could see the truth about people. She

looked beneath Mr. Gagney's smiling exterior, and what she beheld was not a pretty sight.

February 26, 1994

Dear Diary,

Gag-Me was here for dinner again. He's here all the time, it seems.

He's asked Mom to marry him.

He bugs her about it every second. The only other thing he talks about is money. How Mom should spend more of it and take trips and "kick up her heels." With him, of course. When he talks about these great trips they could go on together, he never mentions me. Which is fine with me—I wouldn't want to go, anyway.

Mom is different when he's around. It's like she's deaf and dumb and blind. How can she not see what a creep he is?

March 4, 1994

Dear Diary,

I am so mad I think I might explode. Wait until you hear what Gag-Me said tonight. We were at the dinner table. I'd like to know how I'm supposed to eat more and gain weight when looking at him makes me sick.

Anyhow, he was, as usual, telling Mom what she should do. His new idea is that we should sell this house and all the land, including the glen, and make

*it into a housing development. "We," of course,
means Mom and him, when they're married. "Real
estate development, that's where the money is," he
said. Always money, money, money. He wants to call
it a cheesy name like "Creekside Heights," or
something just as stupid.*

*He said we could build roads all through the
meadow and squeeze up to fifty houses between the
road and the glen. I said, "But I like it the way it is.
What about the deer who come to the meadow and
all the birds and animals and turtles and fish in the
glen? What about how pretty and peaceful it is?"*

*He looked at me real cold and squinty, as though
he wished I was a bug and he could squish me, but
with this phony smile, and answered me in that
sticky voice as if I was a moron or something. "But,
Lucy dear, it's that kind of silly, sentimental thinking
that stands in the way of progress."*

He's the moron!!!

*Daddy loved this house. It belonged to his great-
grandfather. And he loved the glen, just the way I
do. Why should we move? I'd rather die!!!*

Oh, Lucy, thought Allie. You don't mean that.

Seventeen

Allie read quickly through the entries for March and gasped when she came to the end of the month. "Oh, no," she whispered.

March 29, 1994

Dear Diary,

I have the worst, most horrible news. I can hardly even stand to write it down, as if seeing it in words will make it really, truly true.

Mom is going to marry Gag-Me.

Gag-Me had his arm around Mom when they told me, as if she was something he owned. He said that things were going to be different around here from now on, because he was going to be my new daddy.

Fat chance, I almost yelled. You can marry Mom, but you'll never, repeat NEVER be my daddy.

I hate him. And he hates me, no matter what Mom says and no matter how hard he tries to hide it.

Mom tried to make everything seem happy and nice. She said one of the things that's going to be different is that we will move to a brand-new house. "Won't that be wonderful?" she said. I said, "No!" Then she looked real sad and hurt and I felt bad. But I was only telling the truth. It's NOT wonderful. It's the worst, most horrible thing that could happen. And I'm not moving and leaving this house Daddy's great-grandfather built so HE can build his crummy houses all over the glen.

I think he's a wicked sorcerer and he's put a spell on my mother and I know why. Money. That's all he wants. He doesn't care about Mom, and he sure doesn't care about me. What he cares about is our money and all the money he can make from selling OUR land.

And I'm going to prove it to Mom somehow.

Before the wedding, which is supposed to be in July.

I don't have much time.

Wow, thought Allie. Quickly, she read through the remaining entries, concentrating on the days when Lucy wrote about the worsening situation with Raymond Gagney.

April 1, 1994

Dear Diary,

This morning I woke up wishing Mom would come in and say "April Fool, honey! It was all a joke. I'm not really going to marry that disgusting man." But of course she didn't.

So I'm keeping my eyes and ears open. Gag-Me has set up an office in the den downstairs, where he does all his big real estate deals. It's not that I eavesdrop exactly, but sometimes I can't help hearing him talking on the phone. I don't understand a lot of the business stuff. But today I heard him say, "Look, the money is no problem. I'll have plenty of it soon." Then the other person must have said, "When?" 'cause Gag-Me said, "July."

The wedding is in July. Do you think that's a Mere Coincidence, Dear Diary? I don't.

April 19, 1994

Dear Diary,

What a totally rotten day. Mom and I went shopping to buy the dress I'm supposed to wear in the wedding. The dress is okay, I guess, but I couldn't even pretend to be excited about it. Mom asked me what was wrong and why couldn't I be happy for her and all that stuff. So I decided to tell her the truth: that I think Gag-Me is marrying her for her money.

First she started talking about Daddy, and how he

would have wanted her to get married again and not be lonely all her life, and I said, "THAT'S NOT IT! I don't want you to be lonely either. I just don't want you to marry HIM." Then I told her he's a phony and slimy and his eyes are cold as a fish's and he gives me the creeps. And she said I wasn't being fair to him and then she cried and it was awful.

She says she loves him. All I can say is, being in love makes people stupid. I have to find a way to wake her up before it's too late.

April 30, 1994

Dear Diary,

Uh-oh. Today I was walking past Gag-Me's office and I heard him talking and he sounded mad. He said, "What do you mean, you can't wait until July?" I stopped walking and stood outside and listened. "I told you, July 14ᵗʰ," he said. Which just happens to be the date of the wedding. Then he said, "All right, all right. I'll take care of it. But it means I'll have to get her to—" and all of a sudden he was at the door and there I was. I tried to act casual, as if I'd dropped something in the hallway and was looking for it, but I don't think he believed me. If looks could kill, I wouldn't be writing this now. I didn't get to hear any more.

Of course he told Mom I was a sneak, and she said, "Why can't you two get along? Why do you keep putting me in the middle?"

It's hopeless. I'm trying to save Mom and she acts as though I'm trying to ruin her life. But I've got to be more careful.

A feeling of dread began to creep through Allie. She was so caught up in the events of Lucy's life that she almost felt as if they were happening to her. She was disgusted by Raymond Gagney, and frustrated at Lucy's mother's blindness.

Yes, Lucy, she urged. Please be more careful.

Eighteen

May 3, 1994

Dear Diary,

Tonight I was watching TV and Gag-Me and Mom were talking in the other room. Suddenly I heard Mom say NO kind of loud.

That's what got my attention, 'cause she usually doesn't say no to him. I started listening. He was acting all lovey-dovey, smoochy-smoochy, saying, "Please, honey, just sign it."

And she said, "I'll have to think about it."

And then he acted real hurt and said, "You don't trust me," and she said, "Of course I do, but I think you should finance it with your own money," and he said, "How am I supposed to be successful if you

don't have confidence in me?" and Mom said,
"Lucy's father left the money for her, so I can take
care of her and educate her. I wouldn't feel right
risking her inheritance in a real estate deal." He said,
"But there's no risk! This is a sure thing! You'll get
the money back twenty times over."

Mom said, "But John left the land to Lucy, really.
And she told you she doesn't want to sell it. You
know how she feels about that glen. It was a special
place for her and her father."

Like Gag-Me cares! Anyway, it went on and on
and finally Mom said, "Let's watch TV with Lucy,"
and he sat there and sulked like a little baby, I swear.
But I was thinking, Good for Mom!!!

May 16, 1994

Dear Diary,

I think I'm onto something BIG!!! Today I went
into Gag-Me's office to see if there were any paper
clips in the desk. It's not that I was snooping or
anything. I mean, it's our desk he's using. And in the
drawer I found sheets of paper covered with my
mom's signature. Except she didn't write it. Why
would she practice writing her own name? It was
Gag-Me, writing her name over and over and over!
There were some old checks there he must have been
copying from. And he was getting pretty darn good
at forging her signature.

So I kept looking around. I know it's bad to peek

at people's private stuff, but I figure this is war. There was a big bunch of papers from a bank in Rhode Island with all these blank lines for "Co-signer's Signature." They were marked with red X's.

Those must be the papers Gag-Me was trying to get Mom to sign. And since she wouldn't, he's going to sign them himself! Which means he's going ahead with his crummy project, promising the bank our money and planning to sell our land!

I have to show Mom. He didn't actually forge her signature on the papers yet. But it's pretty obvious what he's thinking about. Oh— Mom's calling me. More later—

Bad news. I left you out on my desk when Mom called me. I thought I'd be right back, but she wanted me to go to the store with her. Darn! Darn! Darn! I can't believe it—I've been so careful to hide you up until now. When we got home, Gag-Me was here and—this is the bad part: I'm pretty sure he found you and read everything I've written.

He was upstairs when we came home, where he doesn't really have any business being. I mean, he doesn't live here.

You were over near the corner of my desk. That's not where I left you.

But the worst thing was the way he looked when he came downstairs. He watched Mom and me real hard for a minute, as if he wondered if I'd already told her what he's up to, and then he stared at me for the longest time, and his eyes were— Oh, I can hardly describe how they looked—dark and empty and cold. It was like looking into a deep, poisoned well.

I've never liked him, Dear Diary, you know that, but I wasn't afraid of him. Until now.

May 17, 1994

Dear Diary,

I told Mom about the papers, but when we looked in the desk they were gone. Mom cried and said she doesn't know if it's true or if I'm making it all up. She said, "Why don't you think he was just doodling?" Then she said, "He didn't actually sign the papers, did he?" Which makes me mad because why doesn't she believe me? Why does she take his side?

Then she said that, either way, she doesn't see how she can get married. Which should make me happy, I guess. But I just feel crummy.

She told Gag-Me the wedding is off, at least for now. She didn't say anything about the papers or her signature or any of that. She just said they had to wait until he and I could get along. He said, "You're going to let that br—" he almost said _brat_ but caught himself in time—"that _child_ decide if you should get married or not? Did you ever consider that she's jealous of me and will do anything she can to prevent the wedding?"

111

And then Mom asked him to leave, and he tried to apologize and make up, and she said she was tired and they would talk about it tomorrow.

And at that moment I was sure I could read his mind. He thinks I'm ruining all his plans. He thinks everything would be perfectly fine if I wasn't around. He wishes he could get rid of me.

I remember his eyes and the way they looked at me, and I think he <u>would</u> get rid of me if he could figure out a way to do it. If he thought he could get away with it.

I'm scared.

Allie put down the diary with shaking hands. That was Lucy's last entry. She died the following night.

Nineteen

Allie sat at her desk for a long time, thinking. Mr. Curtis's boss was looking for a red leather diary that matched Allie's journal. Mr. Curtis's boss was upset that the diary hadn't been found. Why? *Because Mr. Curtis's boss was Raymond Gagney!* And Gag-Me didn't want anyone to read what Lucy had written about him!

Allie glanced at the clock. It was 7:30. She raced downstairs and hollered to her parents, who were in the living room, "I've got to go to Dub's for a minute to get a homework assignment. I'll be right back." She crossed her fingers as she lied. She felt bad about it, but she was in too much of a hurry to try to explain to her parents where she was really going.

"Okay, sweetie," her mother called, "but come right back."

Allie got on her bike and pedaled furiously up Cumberland Road, turned onto High Street, and headed toward the Stiles house. She stopped in front of the sign for GLEN VIEW ACRES and read the words at the bottom: "R&G Enterprises, Santa Monica, California. Call 1-800-NEW-HOME for information and free brochure."

R&G Enterprises. Raymond Gagney. R and G.

Allie's knees wobbled as she turned her bike around and rode home. Her mind raced as she pedaled down the street: *Lucy Stiles didn't fall from the cliffs above Fossil Glen: Raymond Gagney pushed her. He killed Lucy and he got away with it.*

She remembered that Mr. Henry had said that Lucy's mother moved to California after Lucy's death. R&G Enterprises was in California. Perhaps, thought Allie, Gag-Me followed her there and sweet-talked her into getting married, after all. And now, at last, Gag-Me was carrying out his plan to develop Fossil Glen.

Allie crept into the room her parents used for an office and dialed the operator. "Could I please have the area code for Santa Monica, California?" she asked. When she called Directory Assistance in Santa Monica and asked for the number of a Raymond Gagney, she was told that the number was unlisted. Next she asked if there was a number for a Rebecca Stiles, but was told no, there was no such listing.

Taking a deep breath, she dialed 1-800-NEW-HOME. "Hello, R&G Enterprises," chirped a cheery woman's voice.

Allie wished she'd planned more carefully what she would say if someone answered. "Um, hello," she said, trying to make herself sound like a woman rather than an eleven-year-old girl. She decided to take a wild chance. "May I please speak to Mr. Gagney?"

"Mr. Gagney isn't in at the moment," said the voice. "May I take a message?"

The woman sounded friendly and helpful enough, so Allie said, "Well, I'd really like to speak with him about Glen View Acres."

"Oh, yes, the project in Seneca, New York."

"Is there a number where I could reach him?"

The woman laughed. "You're in luck, honey. He's there now. I'll give you the number of the New York office and you can try him. Although you probably won't be able to reach him until tomorrow. It's still business hours here on the West Coast, but it's what—a little after 8 p.m. there in New York?"

Allie glanced at the clock. "Yes," she said.

"Well, here's the number." The woman read off a number and Allie copied it on a notepad.

The telephone exchange was familiar; Allie recognized it as that of a nearby town. Good, she thought. It's not a toll call. She dialed the number.

To her surprise, a man answered after two rings.

"Hello," he said brusquely.

"Hello," said Allie. "Is Raymond Gagney there, please?"

"Speaking."

Allie felt a moment of panic. Gag-Me himself! The man who came so horribly alive in Lucy's diary, the man who had killed her! Without thinking, Allie blurted, "I have the book you're looking for."

There was a pause. "Who is this?"

"I know what you did to Lucy," Allie went on, unable to stop herself. "You'd better not sell the glen, or you'll be sorry!" Quickly, she hung up, then stared at the phone in horror. What if it rang? Could Gag-Me trace the call? What if he had Caller ID? What in the world had she done?

She lifted the receiver again and dialed Dub's number. When he answered, she told him all about the diary and about the call she had made to Raymond Gagney.

"You did *what*?" Dub shouted in her ear. "You called a murderer and said, 'I know what you did'? Why didn't you just say, 'Please come kill me, too'? Are you *crazy*?"

"Geez, Dub," said Allie, "take it easy."

"Did you actually say, 'You'll be sorry'? Oooh, I bet that scared him, Al."

"I never thought he'd answer the phone!" Allie wailed. "So I was sort of—unprepared."

"I'll say," said Dub darkly. "You didn't happen to

say, 'By the way, my name is Allie Nichols and I live at 67 Cumberland Road,' did you?"

"Give me a break," said Allie. "I'm not *that* stupid." There was a silence. "Dub, you're scaring me," she said in a small voice.

"Well, I'm sorry, but I wish you'd called me *before* you got the brilliant idea of calling to threaten a known murderer."

"He's not a known murderer," said Allie. "That's the problem. We're the only ones who know."

"Didn't you tell your parents?" asked Dub.

"I can't," Allie answered.

"Why not?"

"I showed them my journal the first night Lucy wrote in it," Allie explained.

"So?"

"And when they saw the message, 'I am L,' they thought I wrote it myself and made up a story about how the words appeared. Then the next night I heard them talking. They were all worried that I'm a hopeless psychopathic liar or something. They were trying to decide if they should send me to a shrink."

"You're not supposed to call them that," said Dub. "They're psychiatrists."

"No kidding, Dub," said Allie in exasperation. "The point is, I don't need one. I'm telling the truth. But they'll never believe me. I mean, I can hardly believe it myself."

"Maybe we should tell the police," Dub said.

"I've thought about that," said Allie. "Can't you just picture the two of us at the police station explaining that a ghost has informed us that she was murdered?"

"Well, there's the diary," said Dub.

"I know, but it's not really *proof*," said Allie. "It ends with her saying she's scared. *We* know what happened after that because Lucy—or her ghost—has practically told me! She made me have that dream where I saw her falling. She told me to look in the newspapers. She told me to search in the desk until I found the diary. She keeps giving me clues. She wanted me to figure out what happened to her. But who's going to believe that?"

"I see what you mean, I guess," said Dub.

Allie and Dub were both quiet for a minute while they thought about the odd happenings of the past three days. It was apparent that Lucy had chosen Allie to avenge her murder. She needed Allie's help to bring Raymond Gagney to justice and stop him from developing the glen.

And Allie wasn't going to let her down. But she had to figure out what to do.

Twenty

On her way to school the next day, Allie was dismayed to see a bulldozer poised at the edge of the meadow. She stopped and stared. It looked like a huge, menacing yellow creature, with a wide mouth made to scrape off the skin and dig deep into the guts of the earth, and treads designed to obliterate everything in their path. She shuddered, imagining the thing at work.

When she got to school, she groaned as she looked at the blackboard and saw the words: Pop Quiz—Math. She was exhausted. How could she possibly concentrate?

Allie had hardly slept all night, thinking about Raymond Gagney and how she could stop him from carrying out his plan. She'd stared wide-eyed into the darkness, hoping that Lucy's ghost would come to her and tell her what to do. She'd gotten up four times to look in her journal to see if any helpful instructions had appeared. She'd squeezed her eyes shut, hoping to see Lucy's face or hear Lucy's voice. Nothing. It seemed as if Lucy had abandoned her.

Every time she began to feel that she might be drifting off to sleep, an image of Raymond Gagney would appear in her mind's eye. She'd never seen the man, but Lucy's vivid descriptions made him real to her.

He knew who she was. He knew where she lived. He was right outside her door. No, he had climbed up and was peering in her window. No, he was underneath the bed. Yes, he was waiting for her to sleep so he could put his hands around her neck as he had done to Lucy, to silence her forever.

Sleep had been impossible. But now that she was in school, she could hardly keep her eyes open. On the day of a math quiz. Terrific.

As always, it was difficult to tell who felt worse about the quiz, the kids or Mr. Henry. He passed out the pages apologetically and told them to begin. "Read each question carefully and do your best," he said.

Allie read the first question. It was about two trains leaving a station at different times, traveling at different speeds. Which one would get from Point A to Point B first? Oh boy.

She read the question again, then drew a little picture of two trains on her scratch paper. She drew Point A and Point B. She stared at the little trains, willing them to chug to Point B so she could see which one would arrive first. They didn't move.

This is ridiculous, she thought. I've got to wake up and think. I've got to be *logical*. She turned back to the problem with ferocious concentration. There was a formula for calculating the answer; she simply had to remember it.

Slowly, she worked her way down the page, carefully filling in answers with her pencil. Soon she came to a question that made her smile. Mr. Henry put one or two gag questions in every test, just for fun. This time the question was: Who is buried in Grant's tomb? Lucy grinned.

Who is buried in Lucy Stiles's grave? The question came to her unbidden. Answer: *No one.* Lucy's body was never found. Allie tried to remember what she had read in the newspaper accounts about the search. The police figured that Lucy fell from the cliff. Since her body wasn't at the bottom of the glen where she fell, they assumed it had been carried downstream. That was logical.

Then, since it wasn't anywhere along the creek's banks, they calculated that it had been washed out into the lake by the high waters of early spring. Again, logical.

But, thought Allie excitedly, Lucy didn't fall. She

was pushed. By Raymond Gagney. And if he'd tried to strangle her first, the way he had in Allie's dream, maybe he hadn't wanted her body to be found. Maybe he had counted on the police figuring things out exactly the way they did.

Which meant that he must have done something with Lucy's body. Allie thought about that, gazing fixedly into space, trying to picture the scene: A dark, rainy night. A murderer standing on a cliff, staring down at the body of his victim far below in a deep and isolated glen. Hoping her body would be swept away, then realizing the risk if the body was ever recovered.

What would he do?

She felt someone's eyes on her and looked up. Mr. Henry was gazing at her with a worried expression on his face. He pointed to his watch and mouthed the words, "Get to work."

Reluctantly, Allie forced her thoughts back to the quiz. When Mr. Henry called for the papers to be handed forward, she had actually answered all the questions. She even thought she'd gotten most of them right.

Mr. Henry announced that since it was raining, with occasional bursts of thunder and lightning, they would postpone their field trip to Fossil Glen until the following day.

Joey Fratto raised his hand. "Did you see the sign at the glen?" he asked. "About building houses there?"

Mr. Henry looked disturbed. "Yes, I saw that," he said, "and I find it puzzling. My understanding was that the owner, Mrs. Stiles, wanted to leave the glen as it is, for everyone to enjoy. I'm really surprised that she would allow this." He shrugged. "But sometimes people have to do things they'd rather not do."

"We could write her a letter," said Dub, "and tell her we've been learning all about the glen and don't think she should let it be ruined."

He looked at Allie, who shrugged and nodded. It couldn't hurt. She hadn't had any luck phoning Lucy's mother, but perhaps Mr. Henry could help them track her down. Allie was willing to bet that Mrs. Stiles—or Mrs. Gagney, or whatever her name was now—didn't know what Gag-Me was up to.

"That's a good idea," said Mr. Henry. "What do the rest of you think?"

"Yeah!"

"Good idea."

"Let's do it."

"Okay," said Mr. Henry. "Tomorrow during our field trip we'll make a list of everything we see and all the reasons why we think the glen should be preserved."

"Can you bring Hoover tomorrow?" Brad asked.

"Please," begged Julie in a wheedling voice.

"Please," chorused twenty-three other voices.

Mr. Henry smiled. His dog not only had been to school on many occasions but also had accompanied the class on several field trips, including one to a local apple farm, where she'd raced through the orchard and eaten the cores of everyone's apples.

There had been one anxious moment when she had disappeared. When the class found her, she was happily rolling in a large, smelly mound of cow manure behind the barn. Even with all the windows of the bus open, the ride back to school was something none of them was likely to forget.

"Good idea," said Mr. Henry. "I'm glad you thought of it. Hoover will be happy, too, I'm sure. But if I bring her, you'll all have to help me keep an eye on her. I don't think there's any cow manure in the glen, but you never know what she'll find to get into."

"We'll watch her," Julie promised.

"All right," said Mr. Henry. "Miss Hoover will join us. Now, since we won't be going outside, let's go back to the library and continue our research there. I want you to look for field guides that will help us identify the things we see in the glen tomorrow. Let's go."

Allie went straight to Mrs. Foster and asked if she could look again at the newspaper articles about the glen. Dub joined her as she began to reread each entry carefully.

"What are you looking for?" he asked.

"I don't know," Allie answered. "A clue, maybe. Something I missed the first time. Or any mention of Gag-Me."

"Yeah!" said Dub. "If the police were suspicious of him back then, they might believe us if we tell them our theory."

"Maybe," said Allie doubtfully. "If we leave out that we got our information from Lucy's ghost."

"But they have to pay attention to murder!"

"Murder? Ghosts?" said a scornful voice. Allie and Dub looked up to see Karen Laver standing behind them. "Don't tell me Allie's sucking you into her ridiculous stories now, Dub."

"Nobody was talking to you, Karen," said Dub.

"But I heard you," answered Karen. "It says in the newspaper plain as day what happened to that girl Lucy Stiles: she fell. Somebody falls or gets hurt in the glen almost every year. But Allie has to turn everything into a big hairy deal."

"Why don't you go mind your own business," said Dub.

"Gladly," said Karen. "It's bad enough that Mr. Henry has made Allie his little pet. I'm surprised that you're falling for her stupid stories, too." With a disdainful toss of her braid, she walked away.

Allie sat where she was, trying to sort out the confused rush of feelings Karen's remarks had sent flooding through her. What was Karen talking about? She sounded—well, if Allie didn't know better, she'd think Karen was jealous. Once again, Karen had managed to take Allie by surprise, attacking and then retreating before Allie had time to take in what Karen had said, and certainly before Allie had time to think of something to say back.

Looking at Dub, she shook her head in consternation. "I wish I knew why she hates me so much."

"Forget it, Al," said Dub. "It's a game she plays. She doesn't have anything better to do. But we have. So let's keep looking."

They went over every account of the disappearance of Lucy Stiles, but found nothing new and no evidence that Raymond Gagney had been a suspect.

"What now?" asked Dub.

"Well, we can hope that your idea about writing to Lucy's mother might at least stop the bulldozers. But that won't help us prove that Lucy was murdered."

There had to be a way. Allie thought about what she had read and about all that had happened. She reminded herself that she wasn't even twelve years old. But she was alive, she told herself, and strong, and pretty smart. And, for some reason, *Lucy had chosen her.*

She owed it to Lucy to see that Raymond Gagney didn't get away with murder.

Twenty-one

After school, Allie waved goodbye to Dub, who was riding his bike to an appointment at the orthodontist's office. Karen and Pam walked off together, pointedly ignoring Allie. Allie stood for a moment outside the building, thinking. Her mind wasn't on Karen and Pam, however, but on Lucy.

Allie's parents were both at work and Michael was at the baby-sitter's, so there was no reason to go straight home. Dub was right: she had things to do. Resolutely, she pulled up the hood of her rain parka and headed over to Fossil Glen.

The day's downpour had slowed to a cold, soggy drizzle as she walked across the meadow. The sky was such a low, dark gray that it felt much later than 3:30

in the afternoon. Wispy fog floated over the tall grass of the meadow and hovered above the deep ravine of the glen, obscuring the edge of the cliffs. Trees seemed to rise eerily out of the mist, only to disappear again in the murky dimness.

Allie wasn't sure she should go to the glen, but she felt drawn to the scene of Lucy's death. She held the vague hope that being at the very place where Lucy had plunged off the cliff would provide a clue or help her know what to do next. And, she admitted to herself, she hoped that Lucy would appear or speak to her again.

Allie stopped near the cliff's edge, or at least what she sensed was the edge. The whole world seemed to be made of the same gray swirling mist. It made her feel oddly off-balance and unreal. She stood peering down. Occasional breaks in the fog allowed her glimpses of the rushing waters of Fossil Creek below.

This was the spot where Lucy had stood right before she fell. Allie pictured Lucy growing too warm in her blue sweatshirt, pulling it over her head, and setting it down on the path, along with the fossils she had found. What had happened next?

Suddenly it seemed to Allie that she was back in her horrible nightmare, the one in which she had felt hands tightening around her neck, the one in which she'd been falling and falling and falling. Once more, the tumbling girl became, not Allie, but Lucy.

Allie felt a strange, menacing presence nearby but couldn't dispel the vision filling her brain. She cringed as the plunging figure reached the ground.

Then the scene in her mind grew darker, as if evening had become true night. Someone was holding the dead girl by the arms, dragging her roughly upstream, grunting with the effort. Allie could make out only his shadowy figure and the sounds of his struggle, which was made more difficult by something he held in his hand.

A noise behind her broke the spell of her horrifying vision. She turned and peered through the mist. She could see no more than a few feet in any direction, except when the fog whirled in the wind and opened like a curtain, allowing her a momentary glimpse through the trees. She saw no one. But there was the sound once more; soft and furtive, like a muffled footstep. And again, closer this time.

The sensation of a menacing presence that she had felt in the dream was with her, only it was real now. Someone was on the cliff path with her.

For a moment she stood frozen, heart fluttering in her throat, eyes wide, trying desperately to see through the haze. She dreaded hearing the next step, but one part of her mind was waiting for it, so she could figure out where it was coming from and run the other way.

There. The snap of a twig and the faint swish of a

branch snagging on cloth. Up the path to the right. Very close.

Why, she wondered wildly, would someone approach with such stealth and caution. Perhaps, she tried to tell herself, the person was lost in the fog, and frightened. Should she call out and announce herself?

"No." It was the voice, Lucy's voice. *"Run. Fast."*

Panic-stricken now, Allie turned and fled down the narrow path to the left. She wanted only to escape, to put distance between herself and those creeping footsteps. Holding her hands out in front of her to help feel her way, she ran stumbling down the wet, slippery trail. Twigs snagged her jeans and whipped her face as she raced blindly forward, the sound of her own flight so loud in her ears that she had no idea whether or not she was being followed. She was far too frightened to stop and find out.

At last, she came to a place where the fog had lifted slightly and she could see the meadow open before her. The ghostly shapes of the school's playground equipment appeared out of the murk. With her breath ripping raggedly from her throat, she ran toward the sliding board and the swing set and the jungle gym. Tears streamed from her eyes, so glad was she to see those familiar objects, looking safe and normal in their usual places.

Only when she was on the High Street sidewalk did she stop and look behind her. She saw nothing but the school grounds and the meadow and the monstrous shape of the bulldozer rising from the low-lying fog like a prehistoric creature.

But Allie knew that someone was there, just beyond her vision, hidden by the mist and the trees. Hugging her rain parka tight to her shivering body, she ran home and locked the doors behind her.

Twenty-two

That night, before going to bed, Allie went from room to room, making sure the windows were closed and latched, and the doors were bolted tight. Her father saw her and asked teasingly, "What's up, Al? Afraid of the Bogeyman?"

Allie looked into her father's kind, laughing eyes and hesitated. How could she begin to tell him she was afraid of a man she'd never met, a man who was a murderer, who had figured out that she was the only person who knew he was a murderer, and that she had found out about it because she'd read the diary of a dead girl? "No," she said finally. Her voice came out funny, high-pitched and quavering. "I was just—checking."

"I always lock up, sweetie. You run on up to bed. It's late."

Allie dreaded going to her room alone. Reluctantly, she turned to climb the stairs.

"Didn't you forget something?" said her dad. He stood with his arms out, and Allie ran to give him a hug. She clung fiercely for a moment before letting go, and he said softly, "Everything okay, Allie-Cat?"

"Yes," said Allie. "I just—"

"What?"

"Just make sure everything's locked, okay?"

"You bet," said her dad, giving her a kiss. "You can count on it."

Allie checked her desk to make sure the diary was where she had left it. It was safe in the secret drawer, which Raymond Gagney obviously knew nothing about. Okay, she thought, he can't get the diary. And Dad locked up the house, so he can't get me. She repeated it over and over to herself: He can't get me, he can't get me, he can't get me.

But even with the lamp on her bureau burning brightly, Allie spent most of the night staring wide-eyed at the cracks in the ceiling, stiffening at every sound she imagined she heard. She longed for daylight, but found that instead of looking forward to the field trip the next day, she dreaded returning to the glen.

She could pretend she was sick. But that was no

good. Her parents would have to go to work, and the idea of staying home alone all day was far worse than going to the glen with her class. She prayed for rain.

She must have slept, because she awakened to bright sunlight streaming through her window. It was a beautiful day. The field trip was on.

Okay, she told herself, she was going back to the glen. What did they say about falling off a horse? You were supposed to get right back on. Besides, she loved the glen. She'd been climbing those cliffs ever since she was a little older than Michael. She wasn't going to let Gag-Me stop her. She got out of bed and dressed in shorts, a T-shirt, and hiking boots.

"Mom?" she asked at breakfast. "Could you drive me to school today?"

"Sure, I guess so. Why? Do you have a lot to carry?"

"My backpack's really heavy," Allie said.

"Okay. Be ready in five minutes," said her mother.

As they drove toward school, Allie looked nervously for signs of Raymond Gagney. She felt a little silly. What was she looking for, anyway? A mysterious black sedan? A lurking figure wearing a raincoat and sporting a bristly mustache? The image her mind created was a combination of Lucy's description and every movie villain Allie had ever seen.

To her relief, no one and nothing out of the ordinary appeared on the way to school. Once in the parking lot, she thanked her mother and ran quickly into the building.

When Allie got to her classroom, Hoover was already there. With a red bandanna tied around her neck and her tail wagging madly, she was prancing happily around the room, sniffing and exploring.

"Hey, Hoover," shouted Joey, "that's my lunch bag!" He grabbed the brown paper bag from Hoover's mouth and gave her a playful pat on the back.

As always, Allie was enchanted by Hoover. She would have loved to own a dog but couldn't because Michael was allergic to pet hair. "Come here, Hoover," she called. "I brought something for you." She reached into her backpack, took out a bag of pretzels, and held them up to show Mr. Henry. "Is it okay if I give her one?" she asked.

"One," said Mr. Henry, "and that's it. The vet said she's got to go on a diet."

"Poor Hoover," said Allie, feeding the big dog the pretzel. Hoover thumped her tail gratefully. Allie rubbed Hoover's long, soft ears and whispered, "No more snacks for you, girl. Doctor's orders."

Mr. Henry flicked the lights on and off and the class grew quiet. Even Hoover sat looking at him attentively.

"Well," he said, "you all look ready for our excursion. Don't forget to bring paper and something to write with and, of course, your lunches. Those of you with field guides, be sure to bring them, too. Do we have one for identifying birds?"

Julie Horwitz held up a book.

"Mammals?"

"Yep."

"Reptiles and amphibians, plants, fossils, trees, and insects," said Dub.

"What about fish?" asked Mr. Henry.

"I've got it," answered Allie.

"Okay, that ought to do it. Everybody ready? Let's go."

As the class trooped across the meadow to the glen, Allie made sure that she was out of earshot of Karen and Pam while she told Dub what had happened to her at the cliffs the afternoon before.

Dub's eyes grew wide. "It's Gag-Me!" he said. "I told you! He's figured out who you are and now he's after you!"

"You think so?" said Allie with a shiver. Then she admitted, "So do I. I've been really spooked ever since. It was so creepy. I'm sure I heard footsteps, Dub. But, I don't know . . . I never actually saw anybody."

Mr. Henry was leading the way down the path to a place where the slope of the cliff was more gradual and easier to manage. Years before, someone had tied a thick rope from tree to tree to form a handrail along a narrow trail that descended to the bottom of the glen.

"Now, take your time and be careful," Mr. Henry warned. "These cliffs are slippery. They're made of what kind of rock?"

"Shale," the class answered in unison.

"Right. And it's very crumbly, so watch your feet."

Allie had to smile at Mr. Henry's caution. He was right, of course. But compared to the cliff she'd climbed earlier in the week, the path was a piece of cake.

One by one, the kids in the class followed Mr. Henry down the hill. Hoover had already raced to the bottom and was splashing in the creek, sending a mallard drake and a great blue heron squawking into flight.

While Allie and Dub waited their turn to go down, Allie walked a little farther up the path to the place where she figured she'd been standing the day before. Sure enough, there were the imprints of her sneakers, clearly outlined in the mud that was beginning to dry after the rain. There were prints where she had stood still, listening, and deep, smeared prints where she had taken off running.

No more than ten feet from where she had stood were several prints much larger than hers.

"Dub!" she cried. "Look!"

Dub ran over and studied the prints carefully. "Well, that proves it," he said. "Somebody was on that path with you. And those shoes don't belong to any kid. Look how big they are."

They stared wide-eyed at each other, neither one saying what Allie knew was in both their minds.

"Come on, you guys," called Brad. "We're leaving you in the dust."

Quickly, Allie and Dub walked back to join the others, glad that it was broad daylight and they were with Mr. Henry and the group and not alone. Most of the kids were already down by the creek, lifting up rocks and peering into pools. Allie could hear Joey's voice booming, "Hey! I found a crayfish!" Julie yelled out that she could see fish near the bottom of the falls.

"I've got the fish book," Allie called back. "I'll be right there."

She and Dub joined Julie on the creek bank near the small waterfall. There, in a clear, deep pool, was a group of fish. They were all facing into the rushing water, swimming so close together that they looked like a big dark mass.

"They're suckers," said Dub.

"Yeah," agreed Allie. "But is that their real name? I'll look them up and find out." She and Dub and Julie flipped through the pages of the field guide and read about white suckers, which each spring swam from the lake up into the streams to spawn.

"Wait, that one over there is different," said Allie, pointing to a larger fish, poised by itself in the shadow of a submerged log. They crept closer to get a better look, and the fish darted quickly to the other side of the pool, flashing silvery stripes on its side.

"A rainbow trout!" shouted Dub. "Mr. Henry! A rainbow!"

Mr. Henry, an avid fisherman, came over to look. "It's a beauty," he said admiringly. "You know, this is one of the few streams around here that's clean enough for trout to spawn in."

"We should put that in our letter to the owner of this place," said Brad.

"You're right," said Mr. Henry. "If they start digging foundations for fifty houses up above, there'll be a lot of erosion from these cliffs. All that mud will make a mess of the stream."

"Hey!" a voice hollered excitedly. "Everybody! Come here! Look at this!"

"Cool!"

"What is it?"

"It's some kind of bird."

"It's a duck, you dodo."

"Oh, yeah? What kind?"

"Where's the book?"

"It's just sitting there! Why doesn't it fly away?"

Mr. Henry, Dub, and Julie headed over to where most of the kids in the class were gathered, looking down at a nest in the crotch of a fallen tree.

Allie continued to stare into the pool at the suckers, distracted by the thought of how awful it would be if the waters of the clear, beautiful pool were muddied and spoiled. Would that mean the fish could no longer spawn? If they couldn't safely lay their eggs here, where would they go? There would be no little baby suckers, no small trout to return to the lake and grow big.

She heard Joey shout, "It's a mallard duck, and no wonder she doesn't want to fly—she's got babies!"

"Come away from there, everybody," said Mr. Henry. "We don't want to bother her."

Allie was starting over to see the ducklings when she noticed that Hoover had strayed from the group and was heading rapidly upstream.

"Hoover!" she called. "Come back here!"

But Hoover, intent on some canine mission, ignored her.

"Hoover!" Allie called again. Hoover disappeared around the bend. "Uh-oh," said Allie. Remembering the cow-manure episode and the class's promise to keep an eye on Hoover if she came along, Allie set off to bring her back.

Twenty-three

Allie ran after Hoover, hopping from one rock to another, trying to watch her feet and at the same time look ahead for a glimpse of the dog's golden fur or the red of her bandanna.

"Hoover!" she called. "Come here, girl." Her hiking boot plopped into the water as Hoover charged ahead, out of sight. Looking down at her sopping foot, Allie muttered, "Mr. Henry should send you to obedience school."

She rounded the curve of the stream and came to a place where the steep shale cliffs widened and the stream bed spread out into a shallow, lazy flow. Bushes, trees, and cattails grew along the edge of the stream, and the ground was softer and spongier and less rocky than farther downstream.

There was a fresh cut in the bank, where the swollen waters had recently washed out a corner. Beyond that was another place where the dirt of the bank was newly disturbed. And there Allie saw Hoover—the back end of her, at least. Her tail was wagging furiously as she dug at the exposed earth bank. Dirt flew backward through the air.

"Hoover, you crazy girl," scolded Allie gently. "What are you up to?"

Hoover looked up momentarily and Allie could see that the dog's face, chest, and front paws were covered with mud. Well, so much for her attempt to keep Hoover clean and out of trouble.

"You're a mess!" Allie scolded. Hoover blinked, unconcerned, and returned to her digging.

"What are you after, Hoovey?" asked Allie. She walked closer, trying to avoid the shower of flying dirt. "Did you find something good?"

At that moment, Allie was overcome by the chilly, shivery feeling that she had first felt at the mailbox. She stopped, waiting to see what would happen next. And it came, a vision in her mind's eye. It was the same scene that had come to her so clearly before: the night of Lucy's murder, the girl's plunge from the cliff, the shadowy figure of a man struggling in the dark, dragging the body upstream—with something in his hand.

What *was* that in his hand? In the darkness of the scene in her mind, Allie couldn't quite see it, couldn't quite make out what it was. She squinted, concentrating. Then, in his struggle to drag the body, the man dropped the object and Allie saw it: a shovel. The image faded away.

Allie stood quietly, considering the significance of the vision. At that moment, she saw that Hoover had stopped digging and was tugging at something in the creek bank.

"Hoover! Come!" Allie called. To her surprise, Hoover gave one last pull and raced triumphantly toward Allie with something in her mouth, which she dropped at Allie's feet. She gave two sharp, excited barks and returned to the cliff, where she continued her excavation.

Allie leaned down and picked up Hoover's offering. It was a ragged piece of cloth, damp and rotten from being in the ground. Gee, thanks, Hoover, she thought. Frowning, Allie examined it and saw what appeared to be a cuff, with the button missing. The sleeve of a shirt, she decided. The cloth was checkered and felt like flannel. The checks were red and black.

With a gasp, Allie dropped the piece of cloth.

The words of the newspaper article about Lucy's disappearance echoed in her brain: *She was last seen wearing jeans, sneakers, and a red-and-black-checkered flannel shirt.*

Horrified, Allie looked ahead to where Hoover was digging deeper into the bank.

"Hoover, *no!*" she screamed.

But Hoover was already running back toward Allie, carrying something long and thin and white, with knobby ends, clutched tightly in her mouth. And although the object was smeared and streaked with mud, Allie knew what it was even before Hoover dropped it proudly at her feet.

Twenty-four

Allie was standing still, staring with fascinated loathing at the bone, when a man stepped out from behind a scrubby willow bush.

"You're a meddler, aren't you?" he said. "Just like her."

With a startled cry, Allie looked up at the figure which had materialized, it seemed, out of nowhere. Although she'd never seen him before, she knew who he was. The thin, bristly mustache and the stained yellow teeth were just as Lucy had described, though he was bigger than Allie had imagined him to be. His face was flushed and sweaty, and he was breathing heavily, as if from exertion.

He wasn't the classic movie villain she had pictured that morning. He was quite ordinary-looking.

Except for the shovel in his hand.

"I can't let you ruin everything now, you realize that, don't you?" He spoke calmly, as if they were discussing the weather, as if he had said, "You realize it's raining, don't you?" He took a step closer, raised the shovel, and held it in both hands like a baseball bat. Mesmerized by his low, reasonable tone and slow, deliberate movements, Allie stood, transfixed. Too late, she realized that he had placed himself downstream of her, blocking any chance of escape toward her classmates.

Vaguely, she was aware of Hoover, running with carefree abandon back toward safety.

Raymond Gagney came another step closer, and Allie took one step back. Again and again, he moved forward and she moved back in a nightmarish dance. Bringing the shovel over his shoulder, Gag-Me prepared to swing. The placid, almost pleasant look on his face made his actions all the more horrifying. He looked like a man preparing to swing a bat in a friendly back-yard ball game.

Their eyes were locked. Lucy had said that looking into Gag-Me's eyes was like looking into a deep poisoned well. Allie could feel herself being pulled into his gaze and down that well. She tore her eyes away, turned, and began to run as the scoop of the shovel whooshed past her head. She ran blindly, splashing through the water, slipping on the loose shale, sinking in the soft, boggy places, running, running, running, keeping a few steps ahead of the man and the shovel that came slicing and whistling through the air.

Desperately, Allie tried to think. Ahead, she knew, was an old mill site. There the glen narrowed again, the sides closed in, steep and high, and the stream bed ended at the foot of a magnificent waterfall. It was a beautiful—and deadly—trap.

Behind her she could hear Gag-Me's labored breathing, punctuated by curses as he struggled to keep up. When they approached the foot of the falls, she heard him chuckle with amusement. "Where are you going to go now?" he asked.

She looked back. Gag-Me had stopped running and was standing, leaning on the shovel, watching her with a curious grin.

There was nowhere to go—nowhere but up. Allie reached for the skinny branch of one of the trees that struggled to grow in the steep, stony cliff side. Digging in with the toe of her hiking boot, she hoisted herself up, planted her other foot, and grabbed for a fingerhold on the root of a hemlock tree. Again, she pulled herself up, and again and again, slowly scaling the face of the cliff. Looking back over her shoulder, she saw with relief that she was out of range of the swinging shovel and that Gag-Me wasn't even attempting to follow her. He stood below her, relaxed, waiting. Waiting for her to slip and fall, or to give up and come sliding down to land at his feet.

Grimly, Allie held on and looked above her to consider her route. Overhead was a relatively flat shelf; if she could reach it, she could rest a moment and then angle over toward a bunch of weeds and vines that would offer a handhold. Beyond that, she didn't know. She'd deal with it when the time came.

Grunting with effort, she managed to pull herself up to the shelf. She looked back over her shoulder and was surprised to see how far she had climbed. Raymond Gagney was about twenty-five yards below her. His smug grin had turned to an annoyed grimace, probably from the realization that Allie was going to be more trouble than he had anticipated. With a sound of disgust, he threw the shovel to the ground and started up the cliff after her.

Terrified, Allie began to scramble haphazardly toward the tangle of vines. She clutched blindly until her fingers wrapped around a stalk. Too frantic to remember to test its strength, she used it to pull herself up. For a moment the stalk held her weight. Then she felt it slipping right out of the cliff, sending her sliding backward in a shower of dirt and shale. At last, she found a foothold on the shelf again and tried to gather her wits and her courage.

Beneath her, Gag-Me was slowly, determinedly climbing higher and closer. She had to figure out each hand and foothold; all he had to do was follow the route she had chosen. A sob of terror and frustration rose in her throat. No, she told herself fiercely. Don't cry. Don't think about him. You can do this; you've climbed places this steep before. Well, almost this steep. Remember the other day. Pretend you're looking for fossils. Take one step at a time. Test each hand and foothold before you trust your weight to it. Slow down. Don't panic. Don't look back. Keep moving.

With desperate concentration, Allie climbed, no thought in her head beyond her next step and that of the man beneath her. There was no sound except for Raymond Gagney's steady swearing, the grunts of his exertion and hers, and the occasional shower of loose stones and dirt.

Gag-Me's breathing was becoming more and more labored. Allie, too, was near the point of exhaustion, but she made herself push on. And then, to her utter dismay, she came to a spot where she was stuck. Above her was a sheer, blank rock face. There was no place to dig a toehold, nothing to grasp, nowhere to go. Below her, very close, was Gag-Me.

Clinging to her fragile position on the side of the cliff, Allie began to sob with helplessness, fatigue, and fear. Gag-Me was climbing steadily. Soon he would reach her and then he would kill her as he had killed Lucy.

Allie closed her eyes and waited to die.

Gag-Me was very close. She could hear the sounds of his struggle, the scramble of his feet, the clawing of his hands on the rock just below her. She imagined that she could feel his hot breath on the back of her legs, and she waited for his hand to close around her ankle.

Suddenly everything was quiet: no breathing, no falling rock, no slipping shale. Allie felt a familiar chill steal down her neck. She heard Gag-Me draw in a sharp breath.

"No!" he cried shakily. "No!" he repeated in a voice filled with horror. "It can't be! Go away! You're dead! No-o-o-o-!"

Next came a long, drawn-out, anguished scream which seemed to go on forever but which could not have lasted more than seconds, as Raymond Gagney fell more than one hundred feet down the side of the cliff. There was a sickening thud when he hit bedrock, followed by an awful silence. It was broken by what Allie only dimly realized was the raw, strangled sound of her own voice, crying for help.

Twenty-five

"Hang on, Allie. You're going to be all right. Help is on the way. Don't try to move. *Hang on.*"

"I can't."

"You *can.* Listen to me, Allie. *You can do it.*"

The voice was Mr. Henry's. It was calm and soothing, and when she thought she couldn't hold on any longer, it insisted that she could. And she did.

Then more people were speaking to her, from the top of the cliff this time. A rope appeared above her, and a man in a safety harness came down with it. He tied the rope around Allie and said, "It's all over now, honey. We're going up. It's okay, you can let go."

But Allie couldn't let go. Her fingers refused to uncurl from their death grip on the cliff; her feet wouldn't budge from their desperate hold on the rock. Finally, her rescuer gently pried open her hands and wrapped his arms tightly around her. Together, they were pulled to the rim of the glen, to safety.

Allie was carried to a waiting ambulance and placed on a stretcher, despite her protestations that she was really perfectly fine. As she was being loaded into the ambulance, she saw that a crowd had gathered. There were two Town of Seneca police cars and a fire truck, as well as many trucks belonging to volunteer rescue workers from the neighborhood.

One of the policemen walked over and stuck his head inside the back of the ambulance. "Do you know the identity of the man at the bottom of the glen?" he asked.

Allie nodded. "Raymond Gagney," she said. Her voice came out sounding dry and croaky. She cleared her throat and wet her lips. "There's another body, too," she added. "It's buried in the side of the cliff. You'll see. It's where Hoover—she's a dog—was digging."

The policeman's eyes widened in surprise. "Another body?" he repeated. "Do you know who it is?"

"Lucy Stiles," said Allie.

"Lucy Stiles. That sounds familiar." His eyes narrowed with concentration, then his expression turned to one of recognition. He said incredulously, "You mean the girl who fell off the cliff some—what?—four years ago?"

Allie nodded again as the ambulance driver appeared at the door. "We'll be heading to the hospital now, officer," he said.

"I'll follow you," said the policeman. To Allie he said, "I'll need to ask you some more questions after you get checked out by the doctor."

Just then Mr. Henry appeared, breathless from running up from the bottom of the glen. "I'm her teacher," he told the driver. "Okay if I ride along?"

"Get in. Let's go."

Mr. Henry slid into the seat beside Allie's stretcher. He grabbed her hand, and she looked up into his worried face. "How are you doing?" he asked.

"I'm fine, really," said Allie. At that moment the siren sounded its urgent wail. Allie smiled. "I always wanted to ride in one of these things," she said.

Mr. Henry laughed and looked relieved, but he soon became serious again. "Who was that man? And why were you so far up the glen? I feel responsible for this, Allie. I should have kept my eye on you."

Allie shook her head. "It's not your fault," she said. "I was chasing after Hoover."

"Hoover! You mean she's the one who led you into this mess?"

"Not exactly," Allie answered. "I was in it before. But if she hadn't run off, I wouldn't have followed her, and then I wouldn't have known that she'd discovered Lucy's body. So, if you think about it, it worked out."

"Wait a second," Mr. Henry said. "Back up. There's another body down there?"

"It's Lucy Stiles," Allie answered solemnly. "Gag-Me murdered her."

"Gag-Me?" Mr. Henry repeated, looking confused.

"Raymond Gagney," said Allie. "Lucy's mother's boyfriend. Gag-Me was Lucy's nickname for him." At Mr. Henry's look of bewilderment, Allie explained, "See, I found Lucy's diary. That's how I knew about Gag-Me. He murdered Lucy, Mr. Henry. It wasn't an accident at all."

Above the wailing of the siren, Allie told a spellbound Mr. Henry the bare facts about Lucy's death. When she finished, she said, "Lucy was a great journal writer, Mr. Henry. When I read her diary, I felt as if I knew her."

"I bet the two of you would have been good friends," said Mr. Henry. "I told you she was special. And smart, like you."

Allie felt her face flushing. To cover her embarrassment, she said, "I'm so glad she kept that diary. I mean, it helped me to solve her murder. But also, in a weird kind of way, when I read her words, it was almost as if she was talking to me—as if she was still alive."

Mr. Henry nodded. "That's one reason I've been encouraging you to put your thoughts and dreams down in your journals."

"Do you keep a journal, Mr. Henry?" Allie asked.

"Sure do," Mr. Henry answered. He started to say

something else, hesitated, then began again. "Allie," he said, "when I first got to you, when you were still hanging there on the cliff, you said something. Something I'm wondering about."

"I did? I don't remember. What did I say?"

"You said, 'Thank you, Lucy.' Then I thought I heard you say, 'for saving my life.' " Mr. Henry looked quizzically at Allie.

"Oh." She didn't know what to say. How could she explain to Mr. Henry what had happened on the cliff?

"Sometimes," Mr. Henry said quietly, "when it's difficult to talk about something, it helps to write about it."

"The way Lucy did, in her diary," Allie said softly.

The noise of the siren began to fade as the ambulance pulled into the entrance of the hospital.

"How did you find me, anyway?" Allie asked. She was curious, but she also needed time to decide how much, if anything, she wanted to tell Mr. Henry about Lucy's ghost.

"Are you kidding? Your scream came echoing down the glen and we all came running. As soon as I saw you—and the body on the ground—I sent the kids back to school for help, and I stayed there with you. That's when I heard you talking." He paused. "I'd like to hear the whole story sometime, Allie, about you and Lucy."

Allie looked out the window, thinking.

"Maybe in your next journal entry . . ."

"Maybe," she said uncertainly. Then, looking into Mr. Henry's eager, open face, she said, "All right. I'll write the *whole* story." With a grin she added, "You've already read the beginning."

"I kind of thought so," said Mr. Henry, grinning back.

The ambulance door opened and a hospital attendant appeared. Mr. Henry scrambled out of his seat. As Allie was lifted out of the ambulance and wheeled inside, he called, "I'm going to wait until your parents arrive, and then I've got to get back to school. I'm afraid to think of what Hoover might be up to. You take care now. I'll see you on Monday."

Allie waved. "Bye, Mr. Henry. Thanks."

In a little cubicle in the emergency room, Allie was examined thoroughly, even though she tried to tell the doctor that she was okay. Despite her scrapes and her sprained ankle, she really *did* feel fine, except when she thought about being on the cliff with Raymond Gagney. His terrified scream echoed through her head again and again and, worse, it was followed by the horrible thud of his landing.

But what she thought about most were the words Gag-Me had spoken right before he fell.

After the doctor had taken her temperature and blood pressure, made sure she could follow a finger with both of her eyes, and poked her here and there to find out what hurt, her parents arrived, breathless with concern. They hugged her over and over and asked the doctor what seemed like a hundred questions. Then the policeman came into the little examining room and asked Allie to tell him what she knew about the bodies in the glen. Here we go again, she thought. Feeling suddenly tired, she said, "There's a red leather book in my desk at home that will help to explain everything."

"Your journal?" asked her mother in a puzzled voice.

"No," said Allie. "It belonged to Lucy Stiles. It's the diary Mr. Curtis was looking for. His boss is the dead man in the glen."

Mrs. Nichols's hand flew to her mouth and her eyes grew round. "What in the world?"

"You know that man?" her father asked with astonishment.

"Sort of," Allie answered. She looked at the expressions of amazement on the three faces above her, took a deep breath, and prepared to tell her story. Or, at least, most of it.

Twenty-six

Allie was released from the hospital a little after noon. At home, she slept for a while. Later she sat in bed, propped up on pillows her mother had fluffed behind her head. Her parents sat at the foot of the bed, and Michael snuggled right by her side. Although he didn't understand exactly what had happened, he seemed reluctant to let Allie out of his sight. She was happy to have his warm little body next to hers.

Allie took a sip of the sweet tea her dad had brought on a tray. She looked gratefully at her family. "I'm really okay, you know," she said. But she had to admit that it felt good to have so much care and concern lavished on her.

Michael reached for the afternoon edition of *The*

Seneca Times, which Mr. Nichols had brought into the room. "Look, Allie. It's you!" He pointed to a front-page picture of Allie being lifted out of the glen by a rescue worker.

Allie looked at the headline: MAN DIES, GIRL RESCUED, BODY UNCOVERED AT FOSSIL GLEN. She set the paper aside. She didn't feel like reading the article just yet.

"Oh, I can't bear to look at that picture," said Allie's mother with a shudder. "When I think—" She broke off and reached over to hug Allie once again.

Allie swallowed hard as she, too, imagined what could have happened in the glen.

"My brave little Allie-Cat," said her father, stroking her hair.

The telephone rang, and Mr. Nichols went to answer it. He came back to Allie's room and announced, "That was the police. They're coming over for the diary."

"I'll get it," said Allie, starting to get up out of bed.

"You're supposed to stay off that ankle, young lady," said her mother. "Let me get the diary."

"I'll be careful, Mom," Allie said, hopping on one foot across the room. "I've got to get it myself. You'll see. It's kind of tricky."

Her parents and Michael watched as Allie pounded twice on the top of her new desk. When the hinges popped open, Allie reached into the secret compartment and took out Lucy's diary. As she held it up for them to see, the doorbell rang.

"The police!" said Michael excitedly. He ran downstairs to open the door, followed by his father.

Allie handed the journal to her mother. Maybe it was the little blue pills the doctor had given her, or the aftermath of the morning's excitement, or the relief of handing Lucy's journal over to the police, but she suddenly felt exhausted. She hopped slowly back to bed, curled up beneath the covers, closed her eyes, and almost immediately fell sound asleep.

That evening, Dub stopped over. Mrs. Nichols told him to go on up to Allie's room.

"Al? Are you all right?"

"Hi, Dub." Allie sat up in bed. She was awfully glad to see him, even though she felt a bit embarrassed to be wearing her old pink pajamas with little purple ponies all over them. "Yeah, I'm okay," she replied. "Mom and Dad are treating me like an invalid, but I'm really fine."

"Michael told me the *police* came."

Allie smiled. "Yeah. Michael thought that was really cool."

"What did they want?"

"They came to get Lucy's diary. They'd already asked me about a million questions at the hospital."

"Did you say anything to them about—you know . . ."

"What?"

"The *ghost*."

"No."

"Good thing," said Dub, with a sigh of relief.

"I almost did," said Allie. "But then I tried to imagine explaining it . . . So I just told them about the diary and kept quiet about the other stuff."

"Did you tell them about Gag-Me following you to the glen after school yesterday?" Dub asked.

"I said I was pretty sure he was there. I told them to look for those footprints we saw. They asked why he would have been after *me,* and I had to tell about calling him, and what I said. My mother nearly had a heart attack when she heard that."

"I can imagine," Dub said dryly.

"The police aren't sure whether he actually knew that I was the one with the diary. My mom bought all that furniture from the Stiles house, so they think he might have figured it out. Anyway, they said the diary by itself wouldn't have been enough to prove that he murdered Lucy. Without a body, Gag-Me could have said the diary was nothing more than Lucy's overactive imagination." She stopped to grin at Dub. "We all know about girls and their overactive imaginations. So getting rid of the body was even more important to him than getting his hands on the diary."

"So that's why he was at the glen, to get rid of the body?" Dub asked.

"Yeah."

"And you discovered him in the act!"

"Yeah. Hoover took off, and I was trying to get her to come back."

"I was wondering where the heck you'd gone when these loud screams started echoing down the glen. Geez, Al, talk about bloodcurdling. You scared us to death."

"You think *you* were scared!"

They were both quiet, remembering.

Allie broke the silence. "The police called again a while ago. They tracked down Lucy's mom out in California to tell her about finding the body and all, and guess what? Gag-Me followed her out there after Lucy died and got her to marry him somehow."

"Yuck," said Dub.

"I know. And guess what else? She never signed any papers saying he could sell building lots in the glen. She didn't know anything about it. She said she told him a couple of weeks ago that she wanted a divorce. So he probably figured this was his last chance to make his big deal."

"Wow," said Dub. "He almost got away with it."

"And guess what else? She called here while I was asleep and talked to my mom."

"Lucy's mother?"

"Yeah. She said she wanted to thank me and all. I guess Mom told her the whole story, including how upset we all were when we saw Gag-Me's FOR SALE

162

sign. Anyway, Mrs. Stiles said she was going to make sure the glen can never be developed. She's going to make it a nature preserve or something, and name it after Lucy."

"Cool!" said Dub.

"I know. Mr. Henry will be glad when he hears that. Oh, hi, Mom."

Mrs. Nichols was standing at the door, holding the portable phone. "It's Karen, sweetie. Shall I have her call back later?"

Allie hesitated. "No," she said. "I can talk now, I guess."

Her mother handed her the phone and left. "Hello?" said Allie.

"Hi!" Karen's voice was breathless with excitement. "Did you see the paper? You're on the front page! There's a huge picture and a whole big article!"

"Yes," Allie answered. "I saw it."

"It's so awesome, discovering a murder! Everybody's talking about it."

"Mmmm," said Allie, curious to see what it was that Karen wanted.

"It must have been so gross to have that guy die right before your eyes."

"Actually," said Allie, "I didn't see him die."

"Whatever," said Karen breezily. "It's still totally gross. Did you see that girl's body? Was it like really, really disgusting?"

"All I saw was a bone," Allie said.

"Ewwww!" Karen shrieked with horrified delight. "And what about the guy? He murdered her, right? How did he do it?"

"Why do you want to know?" asked Allie.

"Why? It's like the biggest thing that's ever happened around here."

"You didn't seem too interested yesterday," said Allie. "You said I was making the whole thing up."

Karen laughed. "Oh, Allie! Don't take everything so seriously! Pam and I were just kidding around. So tell me, how did he kill her? Do you know?"

"Yes," said Allie. "I do. But if I'm such a liar, how do you know you can believe me?"

"Allie, *come on*. Lighten up! Can't you take a *joke*? You're such a party pooper sometimes."

Allie was silent.

"Hey," Karen went on. "I know! Why don't you come over tonight? Pam's sleeping over. We can watch the season finale of *Teen Twins*. The previews looked really awesome."

Allie almost smiled. Two days before, she would have jumped at the chance to spend a Friday night at Karen's house. But now she said, "I can't, Karen. I've already got a friend over—Dub. But thanks, anyway."

No sound came from the other end of the line. Allie imagined the look of surprise on Karen's face. "Well, I've got to go," Allie said. "I'll see you Monday, Karen. Bye."

She clicked the phone off and looked at Dub, who had been listening, eyebrows raised. "What?" she said.

Dub shook his finger at her, making a tsk-tsk sound. "Queen Karen isn't used to having her loyal subjects dismiss her."

Allie shrugged.

"Let me guess," said Dub. "Now that you're a big celebrity, she's acting like your best friend again. This afternoon I heard her telling everybody that you told her *all* about Lucy's murder yesterday, but that she had promised not to say anything."

"I can't believe it. Yesterday she wouldn't even talk to me." Allie shook her head in amazement. "How could I ever be so dumb as to think she was my friend?"

Dub tactfully said nothing.

"Well, I think I've figured something out," said Allie.

"What?"

"When you start to see ghosts and hear voices—*that's* when you find out who your friends really are." She looked down at her hands on top of the covers, embarrassed to look at Dub. After a minute, she glanced up to find Dub grinning at her. "Okay," she said, "I admit it. You were right about Karen. And Pam, too, I guess." She grinned back. "I really hate it when you're right."

"I can't help it," said Dub with false modesty. "Being right is what I do."

"It's weird," said Allie, speaking her thoughts out loud as they came to her. "Sometimes I see things other people don't notice—"

"Yeah," said Dub, interrupting. "Like ghosts!"

"But," Allie went on, "other times, the truth is right in front of my face and I don't see it. I mean, I kept trying to figure out what I was doing wrong to make Karen and Pam not like me, and it wasn't my fault at all."

"You *were* a little dense on that one," Dub said. "But you caught on." He shrugged. "Nobody's perfect."

"Gee, thanks," said Allie wryly. She picked for a moment at one of the bandages on her hand, then said, "I'm kind of sorry it's over."

"What do you mean?"

"I'm going to miss her."

Dub looked incredulous. "Karen?"

"No, silly. Lucy's ghost."

"I thought you said it was scary having her around."

"It was, at first. But then it was so exciting."

"If you ask me, it got a little *too* exciting this morning," said Dub.

Allie laughed in agreement.

Dub thought for a minute and said, "She probably won't be back, you know. I think she got what she was looking for."

Allie nodded. "Dub, she saved my life. When I was on the cliff and Gag-Me was about to catch me, I was sure I was going to die. I think I would have, too, except all of a sudden I heard him say, 'No! It can't be! Go away! You're dead!' And then he screamed and—fell."

Dub's brow wrinkled in concentration. "You think he was talking to Lucy?"

"Who else?"

"You think he saw her?"

Allie nodded. "I think she appeared to him and scared him—to death."

Dub looked impressed. "Wow." Then he said, "What do you think will happen now?"

"Well, the truth is out now about Lucy's murder. Gag-Me's dead. Lucy's mom is going to protect the glen. I guess Lucy's ghost can go wherever spirits go to rest in peace."

"So now everything is going to go back to normal." Dub sounded disappointed.

"Oh, I don't know about that," said Allie. She hesitated, then remembered: this was Dub. "What's *normal*?" she asked.

Dub laughed. "Good question."

"There's no telling what might happen next."

Dub said teasingly, "Oh, like maybe another ghost will come along tomorrow, needing your help."

"It might," said Allie. "I'll be ready, just in case."